MW01264729

WANTED: A BOYFRIEND WHO DOESN'T SUCK
-BOOK 3-
THE DREAM PRINCE
By
Natasha Sapienza

PART 3
THE DREAM PRINCE

1. THE DREAM

Today is the first day I haven't cried once.

I closed my Bible and put it back on my headrest. My weary eyes traced the fluffy afternoon clouds floating in the distance outside my window. I can't believe I'm already finishing the book of John. I blame skipping college and working only six hours a week teaching musical theatre and drama classes at Honey's. A blessing, despite the fact that Dace also still works there. I smiled as I rested my head on my pillow. I can actually think of him now without drowning in tears. From six days ago, the night Dace chose his dreams over me, and I cried out to God until yesterday, I've been crying less and less. Every instance I almost lost it, God did something supernatural...

I was sweeping the TV room two days after the devastating heartbreak, minding my own business when the image of Dace's broken countenance and dead eyes rattled my brain, and a wave of agony slammed over my heart.

I'd dropped the broom and began crumbling to the floor. But the TV was on. I had it to a Christian worship music channel (legit ALL I've been listening to since that dreadful night), and a man's soulful voice began speaking to me. *One of the most difficult things to do is find yourself in a storm. And while in that storm, it seems like everyone who you thought you could count on has walked away. And sometimes, it seems like even God Himself has forgotten about you, but in spite of that, to still be able to lift your hands and say, "Lord, I trust You..."*

From my parents hard, tile floor, I peered up at the screen: James Fortune & FIYA, I Trust You.

My ears perked up, the tears and pain still flowing. Every word spoke of trusting the Lord, despite feeling alone, despite the pain, despite the thoughts. Over and over again those words, "I trust You." My tears slowed, the wrench in my heart unclenching. A smile replaced the ache inside and I took in a slow, steady breath. Yet again, the Unseen One saw me.

It blows my mind. Six days ago I was shattered, crying as if my mom had died, and now here I am, with a smile on my face before I go to sleep. My gaze found the Twilight poster of Bella and Edward, still hanging on my wall. Maybe now that I'm putting You first things will work out with Dace. Or maybe Chris will come back…

"You know what God?" I spoke aloud to my King. "Forget about Dace and Chris. I wanna dream of a new guy." I pulled my covers up to my shoulders and then drifted into another land…

Nighttime loomed over the dark alley, wet from a recent rain. I slipped my hands into the pockets of my sweater as I walked down the thin walkway. The damp ground magnified the sound of my footsteps as they collided with puddles. I drew near to a dumpster, the air suddenly colder.

"Boo!" A dark haired man in a gray trench coat emerged from behind the dumpster, blocking my path. He grinned as he stepped closer, his empty black eyes like a shark's.

Fear gripped my soul as I inched back, gazing at his fangs. Slipping on the pavement, I tumbled to the ground. The vampire propelled forward like a pouncing lion, his long arms reaching for my neck. A cloaked person fell from above and landed in between us. Their fist slammed into the vampire's face, sending him flying backwards. The moment he hit the ground, the hooded person swooped down on him.

Removing a stake from under their cloak, they stabbed the vampire in the heart. His body burst into ashes and soon nothing, but debris remained. The person looked back at me, lowering their hood. A gorgeous young man with black hair that fell halfway down the sides of his cheeks peered at me with clear, light eyes.

"Thank you," I said.

He smiled, his teeth revealing fangs.

Light penetrated my eyelids, coaxing me awake. I lay swaddled in my burgundy comforter in the warmth of my bedroom. I turned toward the Twilight poster of Edward and Bella, smiling as I thought about my new and mysterious dream boy.

2. ANSWERED PRAYER

"I'm worried about you." Mom, in a plaid jammy dress that hung like a tablecloth on a clothesline, with her blonde hair in a haphazard bun, stopped washing the dishes and turned to me as I sat on a stool at the island, a piece of fresh Cuban bread in hand.

"Mamatu, there's nothing to be worried about."

"Mama says it's just a phase, that you get fanatical about things and then a few months later it dies out."

"A phase?" I put the soft, scrumptious bread from my people down. "Mom, it's God, He helped me. For once in my life I'm completely happy—and I'm single!"

"I don't know, Mamashmoo. You're being a little…obsessive."

"What, because I'm finally reading the Bible you gave me when I was eight? I mean, really, Mom, I can't explain how He makes me feel, how He mended my heart, but know that I'm fine, okay?"

She frowned and then nodded, her worry still plain as the morning brightness outside our living room window.

I slipped off the stool and hugged her. "And I won't be over Him in a few months."

I trotted upstairs and into what used to be my room, but is now the computer room, and sighed as I sat down at the desk. No one in this house understands. Even Dad seems like he hardly does, although he's been going to church every Sunday for the past eight years. He's been quiet about the whole thing, like he usually is when it comes to my relationships, but at least he's not concerned for my sanity.

"Lord, I need a friend. Someone who understands." I logged onto my Facebook and skimmed my updates: new friend request: Kelly Rover. Kelly from elementary school? I clicked on her picture. Still with pin-straight, brown hair and a round, pretty face with that dimple on her chin, she beamed in her profile pic like she'd hit a jackpot. Her description read: *A woman's heart should be so lost in God that a man has to pursue Him in order to find her.*

My heart somersaulted. No. Way.

I swiftly scrolled down.

School: FSU

Religion: Jesus isn't about religion. He's about relationship. A relationship that changes you.

Oh my gosh! She's a Christian! Score! I pounded my keyboard, my heart hitting as fast as my fingers.

Hey, Kelly! It's been a long time. How have you been? We should hang out whenever you come down. Write back please!-Natasha.

I grinned. This is crazy. The last time I saw Kelly was in eighth grade at a party and she, like myself, was definitely not a Christian. Or at least not very mature in our faith...Booty dancing since the third grade...Lord, have mercy.

My phone vibrated in my pocket. "Hello?"

"Hey, Tash, what are you up to?" My girl, Marilyn.

"Nothing much, on Facebook."

"Want to go to the mall?"

I looked at the time, 7:34pm. I have been cooped up inside all day. And it would be nice to get out and be away from my worried mom. "All right."

"Okay, I'm leaving my house now. I'll be there in ten minutes."

"'Kay, see you soon."

"Peace!"

I logged off Facebook and shut down my computer. I wish Kelly was on now. I wanna know what changed her and how long she'd felt this way. I wanna talk to someone who understands what I'm experiencing. I love my besties, but I literally have no one who gets what in the heaven happened to me. They're super chill about it, but it's like I'm speaking an entirely different language—literally.

My eyes watered. Hopefully the mall will take my mind off of this lonesome reality.

***

Fifties music, hamburger greased air, and familiar faces from high school swathed Johnny Rockets.

Seated at a red booth, I stirred the last sips of my Butterfinger milkshake with my straw, while Marilyn dabbed her last fry in ketchup. Her pretty blue eyes gently scrutinized as she asked for the third time, "So, you really don't want to watch a movie?"

"No, Mar."

"Then…what do you want to do?"

"Honestly, I just want to talk…" About God.

"Okay…" Her face reminded me of Mom's. Thankfully though, she's not as critical. "Let's go outside then."

"All right."

Mar spotted the check for my still, mostly-broke self, and we walked outside to the third story parking garage, taking a seat in the same spot I saw Chris and Christina at a few months ago. A week after we'd told each other for the second time that we loved one another…

The warm night whispered a breeze, gently fanning Mar's brown tresses. "So… you and Dace are done?" She said.

"I think. I mean, we told each other goodbye, and we barely text anymore."

"And Chris?"

"I don't know."

Now her beady eyes studied me like a psychologist patient on a couch. "Why are you upset? None of them are the one. The one is still coming. And he's going to blow them both out of the water."

I sank against the hard railing. Maybe Dace is the one, but now isn't the right time. He said he wanted his dreams more than he wanted me, but people change. Who knows what will happen in the future. We still see each other three times a week at the studio…

Or maybe me and Chris are meant to be, but it isn't the right time for us either. We've always had so much in common, and both of us had dreams of moving to Los Angeles. Although he's not an actor, he loves film and is still an artist. And I'm heavy on signs and it seems like everywhere I go, I hear the kid's name or see a movie he turned me onto...I don't know.

I looked up at the moon. A ring surrounded it...just like the one I saw with Chris! A faint tingle tickled my heart. That place apparently still reserved for Chris... Could he actually be the one?

I sighed. Whatever. This boy talk is lame. "I kind of want to go home."

Mar's mouth twisted. "Okay."

We left that familiar spot with more than one memory of Chris, and walked in silence toward the parking lot. I feel bad, but I'm just not in the best mood. I'm lonely, and what I truly want to express, I can't share with her because she won't understand. She's Jewish by non-religious upbringing, and says she believes in God, but believing in and knowing His Son is something so different. Something I'm still figuring out...

I gazed at the stars. God, I really hope I'm not alone like this for long...

***

After sneaking into the house and dodging Mom and Dad, distracted by a movie in the TV room, I escaped to the office and checked my Facebook. New updates. A message from Kelly! Already? I quickly opened it:

Hey girl! I'm great! I'm actually in Boca right now. I'd love to hang out sometime. Call me so we can make plans. XO!

I swirled the chair around. This is too good to be true! Just a few hours ago I was super down about how alone I am and now me and Kelly are getting back in touch—after both having become Christians—or surrendered ones at least. I dialed the number Kelly gave at the end of her message.

"Hello?" Her sweet voice resonated a hint of Southern twang.

"Hey, Kelly, it's Natasha."

"Hey, girl, how are you!"

"I'm good, how are you?"

"Bored out of my mind."

My chair spinning slowed. Marilyn's sad and perplexed face when I announced my early departure poked my thoughts. "I feel you, girl. We should hang out soon. I mean,

I know tonight is too short notice so maybe
—"

"No, tonight is perfect. My friends were
going to a club, and I wasn't down for it so
I'm totally free. I mean, if you can."

I jumped out of my seat. "Sure! Would
you like to sleep over? I know Boca's kind of
a drive."

"Yeah, that would be awesome! Let me
just ask my mom. Hang on."

"Oh yeah, me too!" I scrambled out of
the room, skipped two steps of our mini-
staircase, and darted into the TV room.
Mom lay across our leather couch, her head
in Dad's lap, who had apparently knocked
out Lord knows how far into the movie.
"Mom, can my friend Kelly sleepover?"

Mamatu raised herself from Dad's lap,
stirring him awake. "Kelly?"

"Yeah, we went to elementary school
together."

She gave Dad one of her cautious side-
looks.

He glanced between the two of us.
"What'd I miss?"

"Natasha wants her friend to sleep over,
but I guess it's fine."

I squealed. "Ahh! Thanks!"

"Okay, hello?" Kelly said.

As Mom continued observing my antics, and Dad continued watching the movie he fell asleep on, I clutched my phone. "Yeah?"

"She said yes!"

I bounced. "So did mine!"

"Awesome! I'll be over there in thirty. Oh, what's your address?"

I spat it out like those game show players racing the clock.

"Got it. I'll see you soon!"

"All right, see you!"

Mom's eyebrow arched as the excitement bubbling inside of me incited my adrenaline. Dad kissed her forehead and rejoined her as my audience of two.

I waved my phone like a prop. "Okay, so I was really feeling lonely because you guys, and Mama, and pretty much everyone thinks I'm crazy so I told God I really needed someone who understands what I'm going through, and I check my Facebook and I have a friend request from this girl, Kelly, who I've known since like kindergarten, but never really hung out with, and I look at her page and find out she's all Christian so I message her earlier tonight and tell her whenever she's down from Tallahassee we should hang out, and when I get home I check my Facebook, and she says she's in Boca and gives me her number, and

I call and say it's probably too late to hang out tonight, but she says it's not, that all her friends were at a club so I asked you if she could sleep over, and you said yes, her mom said yes, and now she's coming!" I sucked in a breath.

Mom's forehead crinkled, her concern for my sanity caked on her face like stage makeup.

Dad rubbed her back. "That's nice, Mama, just try not to be too loud, I'm going to bed soon."

"I got you!" I gave both the 'rents a quick squeeze and then ran back upstairs to my room. I gathered all the dirty clothes I had flung across the floor and threw them in the hallway hamper before making my bed. I reorganized all the jewelry and makeup dispersed along my dresser, and did a final scan of my still Chris-inspired, Asian themed room. Eh, it's decent enough, but I really do need to take better care of this place. You'd think three boys shared it.

Two polite knocks rapped the front door.

"She's here!" I scurried downstairs, jumping over the last three, and opened the door.

Kelly, wearing a small denim book bag and a cozy t-shirt, opened her arms. "Hey, girl!"

"Heyyyy!"

We hugged, Mom approaching us as we let go.

"Mom, this is Kelly."

Kelly smiled, her adorable dimples so innocent and inviting. "Nice to meet you, Mrs. Sanchez."

"Please, call me Marcia."

I gestured to Kelly's bag. "You can put your stuff down in my room."

"Thank you."

Mom, sneaking size-ups, titled her head toward her bedroom. "You girls try to be quiet, okay? Your father's asleep."

"Okay." I tiptoed upstairs with Kelly and led her into my room. I gently closed the door behind her as she set her bag down beneath my paper lantern in the corner.

"I love the beige walls with the one red and then the black dresser and bed frame. It's all Asian."

"Yeah, we finally redecorated and painted the walls after eighteen years."

"Wow. It looks really nice."

"Thanks so much."

Another sweet dimpled-smile appeared as we sat on my bed. "God is really funny," Kelly began. "I was so bored at my mom's house 'cause my friends went out, but I wasn't about to go to a club, so I'm just reading the Word and listening to music, and I'm like, 'God, I just wanna talk to someone about You. I wanna hang out with someone who loves You and knows You,' and I see your Facebook message and here we are."

My mouth dropped open before I replied. "Wow. I was feeling lonely and wanted to talk to someone who's experiencing Him, too, and I saw you wrote back, and I called you and yup, here we are."

As we shared a laugh, I grabbed a pillow and hugged it, settling in for what I've been craving all day. "So when did you come to God?"

Kelly criss-crossed her legs. "Well, to summarize, it had a lot to do with a guy. My dad wasn't really there for me so I became very needy for a man's affection, and I had a boyfriend who was very atheist. I always kind of believed, but one day he asked me why I believed, and I couldn't really answer him. So I decided to find the answer, and I started reading the Bible and going back to church with some friends of mine in Tally, and I just started to fall in love with God. And the more I got to know Him, He revealed to me that being with my boyfriend was pulling me away from Him, but I couldn't bring myself to break up with him.

"Finally, one day my boyfriend went from, 'I love you,' to, 'I want nothing to do with you.' And I mean out of nowhere, and I knew it was God hardening his heart against me."

"Wow…" I tightened the hold on my pillow. So God can harden people's hearts? I wonder…

"Well, at my church they had a prophet, and he told me to stay after service, that God wanted to bless me with a gift. I knew right away what he was referring to. My friend had gotten the gift of tongues, and I wanted it 'cause I wanted to feel closer to God so I had been asking Him for it."

"I read a little bit about tongues in the Bible," I said.

"Yeah. It's basically God's Spirit praying on your behalf."

I nodded although, admittedly, I don't understand the concept too well. I've been devouring my Bible, but I'm still only a quarter into the New Testament.

Kelly continued, her doll like face glowing. "So after service the prophet tells me to close my eyes and just talk to God, like privately. So I do and he's praying and talking with a few others and then comes back to me. And I start feeling something, but I'm like freaking out 'cause I didn't want to end up like those people who fall to the floor and start yelling out in tongues. And the prophet's like, 'I can see the Spirit coming upon you, don't be afraid. Just keep talking to God.' So I do, and I'm like, 'God please help me, I want this gift, but I'm afraid.'

"But then I start to feel lighter, and this peace growing inside me, and I start thanking God for His goodness and my mouth opens and I'm like mumbling. And then the prophet comes back and lays his hand on my shoulder, and I just started speaking in tongues and it was like this amazing feeling of peace and love and like air rushing through my entire body like I've never felt before. It was amazing. I wish I could feel like that forever." She smiled, her brown eyes gleaming. "Well after that experience I completely fell in love with God, and just continued to pursue Him to this day."

"Wow." I shook my head. "I wanna meet a prophet. They can like, tell you things right?"

"Yeah, they can give you a word from God, even about your future, but only if

God desires to tell you something through a prophet. It's called getting prophesied over."

I drummed my fingers against the pillow. "I really want to. I've been so confused lately with my exes, Dace and Chris. I still care about them, and sometimes I get signs and stuff about Chris, but I still think of Dace, and it's so frustrating."

Kelly, all peaceful and wise-looking, spoke with such calm confidence. "Pray about it."

"How?"

"Just ask God to place a prophet in your path."

I pursed my lips. My grandma always tried to be some makeshift psychic in my life. Whether it was offering to throw special rocks, or flip some special cards, she'd make guesses about my love interests that sometimes came to pass and other times did not. I'd never come across a Christian claiming to have foresight into my future, but the Apostle Paul mentioned prophets being gifts from God. And at this point, the confusion between if Chris is the one, or if Dace is Mr. Right and it's simply the wrong time, is irksome. But I suppose it's worth a shot.

I eased back against my headrest/bookshelf. "Can you pray that He does, too?"

"Sure."

I smiled at my new friend in Christ, my own gift from God. "Thanks, Kelly,"

She smiled back. "No problem, sister."

3. THE PROPHET

Thank God we didn't see that romantic comedy.

Alice, striding beside me in cherry red, shrugged as we walked out of the movie theater and passed the Johnny rockets. "That movie was good."

I gaped at her. "Good? That movie was awesome!"

"Yeah, but I was still in the mood to see a romantic comedy."

I shook my head as we traversed into the parking lot. Action flicks are perfect for my current predicament. Watching love movies when I'm trying to focus on God—not Dace and Chris—are a big no no.

"Look, it's Marcos," Alice said as Marcos Pantero and his brother, Hector, walked our way, both still rocking the same baggy jeans and big T's they wore in ninth grade.

Oh gosh. I remember when they danced in my fifteenth birthday party…when Alice and Hector were boyfriend and girlfriend.

Marcos grinned as they stopped in front of us. "Hey, hey, look who it is."

I gave them each a quick hug.

Hector smirked as I pulled away, his eyes glued to Alice. "What's up, Alice in Wonderland?"

An uncomfortable smile twisted Alice's pretty face. "Hi."

"Oh, Natasha," Marcos said, "I know you're all religious and stuff now, and there's this 'event' at FIU tomorrow night. Surge and some other Christian boys from Krop are going."

I decided not to correct his 'religious' comment. If I said relationship with God, he'd probably still write me off as a religious nut. "Sounds cool." I turned to Alice. "You wanna go?"

"Sure."

"Just go on his Facebook and get the info," Marcos said.

I gave my old friend and backup dancer a genuine smile. "All right I will, thanks."

"Yeah, well we have to get going. See you girls." He gave us a hug and strode off, but Hector lagged.

"Bye." He gave a hug like his little bro did, but also laid an additional wet kiss on Alice's cheek before strolling inside the mall like he'd just won a basketball game.

"I can't wait to check out this event," I said as Alice wiped her cheek.

"Yeah, it sounds cool."

As I trailed my bestie to her car, I couldn't help but think it rather random that a "non-religious" guy I used to hang with in tenth grade would invite me to a Christian event that he wasn't even attending…

My eyes wandered to the evening heavens above. I wonder…

***

I recognized a few of the tall boys in church suits, huddled together and praying outside the auditorium doors as Alice and I approached. They also went to Krop. Warmth seeped into my heart. It's refreshing to see so many young people into the same God I'm into. I'm really not as alone in this as I sometimes feel.

"Hello, welcome." One of the boys handed us a program as we walked inside.

About two hundred people stood in the rows as a pianist, drummer, and singers began a song. The melody boomed through large speakers on either side of the stage, engulfing the auditorium with praises. I tried to focus on the words, but a thought reigned in my mind. Can it be, that somewhere amongst this large crowd, a prophet stands singing along? Oh, please, Lord, let there be one here. I could use some clarity on the whole Chris and Dace thing. Just the other day, I was at the mall and someone called out, "Chris," just as I passed by. It wasn't him, thankfully, but it's something...

After a few more songs, a man—likely in his late twenties—dressed in a white suit, entered the stage, joining in with the choir. As the song ended, other classy-dressed men and women lined the back of the stage.

The man in white bowed his head. "Lord, may Your presence fill this place. May You give Your people a word tonight. Bless this time now we ask in Jesus' name, amen." He smiled as he gazed at the attendees. "Good evening, you all may be seated. My name is Pastor Aaron, and I want to thank you all so much for being here tonight. But before we go on, I'd like to introduce some special friends of mine." He gestured to a couple standing on the left of the stage and rattled off bishops and worship pastors all the way down the line until the last man seated at the end, short and dark-eyed. "And last but not least, Martin Evans, a mighty prophet of the Lord."

My heart jumped as a man at the far right surveyed Pastor Aaron. Although short in stature, the intensity in his gaze made him seem bigger…stronger.

"There's a prophet here!" Alice whispered.

"I know!" My head spun as Pastor Aaron began to teach, and I forced my eyes off Martin. Oh my gosh, You really did it Lord! I can't believe I wasn't completely confident in this happening. You're so awesome!

I could barely pay attention to the sermon. I just have to speak to that prophet. This is what I've been praying for since the conversation Kelly and I had the night she slept over. I asked for a prophet and now he's here, in the same room as me!

The sermon flew by, somehow catching up with my racing pulse.

"If you need prayer, we will all be here," Pastor Aaron said. "Just come on forward."

People bustled out of their seats, and lines quickly formed on both sides of the stage. Martin, however, miraculously stood alone.

I slapped Alice's bicep. "I'm going for it!"

"Yes, girl, go!"

I beamed as I hopped out of my chair. Alice isn't exactly a Jesus freak, but she is super supportive nonetheless. She knows I've been praying for this, and now she got to witness an answered prayer firsthand.

The noise heightened as I neared the stage. On my left and right, men and women, young and older alike, stood across all of the people Aaron had introduced, talking or praying. I climbed the steps and veered right, toward Martin. His dark brown eyes didn't meet mine until I stopped two feet away from him.

I cleared my throat and the words came pouring out. "Hi, I know you don't know me, but I've been praying for God to put a prophet in my path and"—

He motioned for me to follow him several feet away from the majority. The noise level decreased and Martin's strong gaze penetrated mine. "Right when I saw you, the Spirit of the Lord told me Satan's been confusing you with relationships."

Tears poured down my cheeks, a flock of emotions swarming my heart as he continued.

"He also told me He's going to make things clear for you very soon."

I held both cheeks as if that'd coax my tears. "Thank you."

"Not a problem." He reached in his pocket and removed a card and a pen, and jotted a number on it. "If you ever need prayer or encouragement, feel free to call."

I wiped my soggy face as I took the card. "Okay, thank you again. I'm Natasha by the way."

"Martin. Good to meet you." He shook my hand. Those piercing eyes squinted some and he spoke once more with a confidence that shook my core. "Very soon."

I smiled as I dismounted the platform, my knees shaking and heart now thrumming in my ears. *You're going to make things clear for me in the area of relationships very soon, Lord? How amazing is that? I do need clarity ASAP so I can know what to do, or just move on already.* That last conversation I had with Dace outside of Honey's a few days ago still hadn't reached a conclusion.

The image invited itself into my mind: Dace and I sitting atop the hood of his black Altima beneath the dusk sky. He'd told me how he was thinking about that sermon again, and thinking maybe we could be together after all.

"So, we are going to try again then?" I asked.

Dace laced his fingers together and gave his crooked half-smile. "I'll let you know soon."

Alice waited for me at the end of the walkway, drawing me back to the event and the reality of what I just experienced. "What happened?"

"He spoke to me." I blinked as the tears resurfaced. "God gave me an answer."

4. The Setup

"And then he told me God was going to make things clear for me very soon and he stressed the 'very soon' part." I sat on my bed, jammies on and phone to my ear as I recounted the God-incidence to Kelly.

"How cool is that?" A smile resounded in her voice. "I'm telling you, girl, prayer is powerful."

"Tell me about it."

I can't believe I had the nerve to doubt God. It's like I know He's all powerful, all knowing, and always present, but I can't seem to grasp the depth of His love. The fact that He cares enough to organize me getting together with Kelly, her telling me about a prophet, me meeting a prophet and then God giving him a word specifically for me, blows my mind.

"Tashi!" My sister barged into my room —and her old one—her brown waves wrapped messily in a high bun, and her midriff exposed above a pair of jogging pants. "Get off the phone, I have to tell you something."

"Kelly, let me call you back."

"Okay, sis'."

Natalia plopped onto my bed as I hung up, her eyes pink and glassy—the consequence of too much internet browsing—or something else. "First of all, what's up with you and Jax?"

I refrained a sigh as I leaned back against my bookshelf. Jax. Two grades higher than me, and two lower than Nati, the bad boy eighth-grader who used to smoke weed with her, whom she always forbade me from going out with, had recently reentered both of our lives. Now twenty and cleaned up, he gave his life to Jesus at my church one day, and we'd been friends ever since. And…a little more than that. Sorta.

Natalia's big, beautiful browns eye-balled me. "I heard you guys hung out on Valentine's Day…"

"We did…"

"And?"

"And we held hands, but he was kinda mad at me the whole time."

"Whaaaat? Why?"

I released the sigh. "Well…sometime before that…we kinda…pop-kissed"—

Nati gasped—and grinned. "No you did not!"

"Yeah...but I wasn't really sure about him. For one, Mar crushed on him hard. She thought he was super hot so every time the three of us hung out, it was awkward. Though she swears after he kissed her best friend he was no longer as hot."

Nati gripped her chest. "I wish I had friends like that. But continue."

"Well, he got mad at me because he knew I was on the fence about us, and he told me he didn't want to keep waiting for me. I told him I wanted to give us a *try*, but he found that offensive I guess so he just stopped talking to me after that."

"Okay, good." She smacked her hands together. "Because there's this guy in my acting class, and I just feel like God's talking to me about you two."

I furrowed my brow. Natalia hearing from God? The same woman who hadn't been to church since ninth grade?

"I'm not interested in guys right now, Nati. I'm just trying to focus on Jesus."

She sucked her teeth. "He's adorable! I thought about hooking up with him, but he's way too young, and I'm telling you, I feel like God wants you to be with him."

I blinked at her. "Um…and you're still married."

"Separated. Anyways, he's got these mesmerizing eyes and he's religious like you."

"Gosh, why does everyone keep calling me that? It's a relationship with God."

She rolled her eyes. "Anyways, he doesn't smoke or drink, or even curse. You should come look at his pictures. I already showed him a picture of you."

"What? Natalia!"

"I showed him the one where you look all Angelina Jolie and he said you're too pretty for him. I was like, 'Boy please.'"

Now I rolled my eyes. "I told you, I'm just trying to focus on Jesus. I don't need a guy, Nati."

"Please, just look at a picture, that's it. For me." She pouted, those big browns quite convincing. This is what happens when you have a sister who acts even better than you do.

I groaned. "Fine."

"Great!" She scuttled into the hallway, pulling me along with her.

I dragged my feet as she dragged me into the computer room aka her new bedroom, and sat me down at the computer. "What's his name?" I asked.

"Jonathan Sapienza."

"How in the world do you spell that?"

"S–A–P–I–E–N–Z–A."

I logged into Facebook and searched his name. A black and white picture of a young man with dark tresses, and a strong jaw line appeared.

I crossed my arms. "That's him?"

"Yes, but he doesn't look like that. His hair is different. Click more pictures."

"I can't, his page is private."

She spat out a cuss word. "Just request him. I'll call him and ask him to add you."

I sighed as she dialed his number. This is such a waste of time. I could be fellowshipping with Kelly, or reading my Bible right now and learning more about God and His plans for my life.

"Hey, Natalia, what's up?" A deep and yet soft voice emerged from her speaker.

"Nothing much. Are you on the computer?"

"Yeah."

"Can you go on Facebook please and accept my sister's friend request so we can see your photos?"

I smacked my forehead. Gosh this girl gives way too much information.

"Um, okay. All my pictures are old though."

She tapped her foot. "Whatever, just add her please and thank you."

"Okay, hang on… All right, I accepted."

"Thanks, darling. Let me call you back."

"Okay."

"Toodles!" She hung up and then hovered over my shoulder as I skimmed through his photos. "So?"

"He's cute, but not gorgeous."

"Ugh, you have to see him in person. These pictures don't do him justice!" She called back.

"Hello?" Jonathan answered.

"So, Jonathan, did you get to see my sister's pics?"

"Yeah, but she's way too beautiful for me."

She sucked her teeth again and winked at me. "Jonathan, please. You're going to Anna and the Tropics next month, right?"

"Yeah."

She poked my arm. "Great, you guys can meet then."

I gawked at her. No she did not just try to set up a meeting for us at the opening of her play.

"Hold on, let me put her on the phone." Natalia grinned as she handed her cell to me.

I grimaced before taking it. I would slap her if I wasn't a Christian. I put on a polite voice. "Hi, Jonathan, I'm Natasha."

"Um, hi. Nice to meet you?"

"Well, maybe we will on March 19th, for Natalia's show."

"Great. I guess I'll see you then."

"Okay, nice talking with you. Here's Natalia." I gave the phone back to her and then walked to my room. I seriously need a lock now that Miss Force-Random-Guys-On-You is living one room over again.

"Okay man," Natalia said from her room. "I'll talk to you later. Goodnight." She reappeared in my doorway as I turned my TV on to my favorite Christian music channel. "So, March 19th it is then, on my birthday debut?"

Less than three weeks away…I clutched my hip. "I guess."

She smirked before disappearing down the hall. I love the confidence she has even though every guy she tries to set me up with I never like. But alas, I suppose she could use a little distracting at this time in her life— and lots of prayer.

The lyrics of a song by Rebecca St. James flooded my room as I closed the door behind her.

"Darling did you know that I

I dream about you
Waiting for the look in your eyes
When we meet for the first time…"

Though new to the song, I hummed along, every lyric sweeter than the next: the singer promising to pray for and wait for her future hubby, encouraging him to do likewise, until they meet at the altar, where they'd choose each other always and forever…

I smiled as I swayed to the beat. Same here, sister. Same here.

5. THE ENCOUNTER

Darling did you know that I, I dream about you, waiting for the look in your eyes when we meet for the first time. I hummed the adorable love song as I sat in the hospital lobby, waving my phone around for service. The lyrics ring so true to me now that my hope of meeting the one someday is restored. Just like Rebecca sings about waiting for her future husband until marriage, that's what I plan on doing. No more wasting time on guys who aren't the ones God hand-picked and designed just for me. I'll wait for my dream boy until God is good and ready to bring him my way.

An 'x' still marked my signal picture at the top of my cell's home screen.

I turned to Natalia, sitting beside me chomping gum while immersed in a gossip magazine. "Can I use your phone?"

Keeping her eyes on the page, she handed me her purse.

I dug through the messy bag and pulled out her iPhone. Jonathan's name appeared at the top of the screen in a text conversation from last night.

Pray for my grandma. Natalia wrote. *She's in the hospital.*

I will. Is everything all right?

A tiny flicker rippled inside of me and ignited my fingers.

Hey, Jonathan. What's up?

I stared at the phone for a moment before busying myself with some of Nati's applications. I don't even know why I messaged him. Let him talk to Natalia for all I care. She's married anyway, even though she's set on divorce. I glimpsed at her.

High-heeled boot twitching, short-skirted legs crossed, an amused smirk across her beautiful face, shaded on either side by exotic, brown waves; if she'd been depressed over the impending divorce, she sure put on a good act that she wasn't. But was she?

After a few minutes I checked her inbox. The text I sent Jonathan remained unanswered. Whatever.

"Thanks, Nati." I dropped the phone back in her purse and continued to hum the Rebecca St. James song.

***

"Man, you'd think Mama never even hit her head the way she was giving it to Tio Michael," Natalia said as she looked up the latest star gossip on our computer. I seriously don't understand why she cares so much. They're just people like us who are rich and really popular. Big whoop.

I stretched out across the tiny twin-sized bed Nati's purse lay on. "I'm glad she's doing better. A lot of people were praying for her."

"Yeah, I sent out a mass text message telling people to keep her in their prayers."

I smiled. At least she believes in the power of prayer. I've been praying for her behind her back ever since the night after I cried out to God. Someday, she's going to be a Jesus-loving, non-cussing, abstinent-till-remarriage, purity ring wearin' Christian. I hope…

I grabbed her bag. "Can I see your phone?"

"Yeah, go ahead."

I removed it from the cluttered labyrinth and opened her text messages. Jonathan wrote back.

Hey. Sorry I got back so late. What's up?
Nothing much, man, at my mom's house.'

I sat up. Natalia wrote back? But I was the one who texted him. I felt that strange

flicker in my heart again, and before I knew it, fingers were flying.

Hey, Jonathan, it's Natasha. I'm the one who texted you earlier.

The phone lit up.

Oh hey, Natasha. How are you?

I'm great and you?

I'm good. Hey, can I ask you something?

Su—

"Natasha, are you using my phone for texting?" Natalia hissed at me like a snake who'd just gotten stepped on.

"Um...yeah. I'm texting Jonathan."

"Well I don't have unlimited text. Give him your number and have him text you there."

"Okay, okay." I rapidly wrote.

Natalia said she doesn't have free text. Can you text me on my phone? After punching in my number, I dropped her cell back in her purse.

"Thank you." She returned to her computer 'research.'

I migrated to my room. Sheesh, she never cared when I texted on it before. One minute she's forcing me to talk to Jonathan on her phone, the next she's griping about me doing so. But then again, those text costs do add up. I've gotten Dad ticked off more

than once because of my talkative texting habit.

I grabbed my phone off my headrest. New text message.

Hey, it's Jonathan.

I smiled as I settled onto my bed. *Hi again :) What did you wanna ask me?*

Well, I was just reading some of my old poems and I'm having trouble forgiving…

Hmm. Unforgiveness isn't one of those hard sins to shed for me, thankfully. But, I do know how binding it can be…

The thing with holding onto the past is it's like a ball and chain, a hindrance. It weighs you down and prevents you from truly moving forward with life. But thankfully, there's a remedy: forgiveness. And it's only when we truly forgive a person that we're able to move forward with life and what we're called to do. Jesus said if you do not forgive your brother his trespasses, neither will God forgive you. But thankfully, forgiveness is His forte so just ask Him to help you forgive that person, and He will.

The thing is, I'm having trouble forgiving myself.

Oh. I tapped my chin. I guess there's only one real answer to that. *Turn to Him. Ask Him to help you move on, or to reveal to you a lesson from it. Ask Him to turn those memories into a blessing rather than a curse.*

I guess I can try that…

Take it this way: if God can forgive Saul, a man who rejected Jesus and abused and arrested anyone who followed Him, and then use him later to preach the gospel to the nations, gifting him with the Holy Spirit, He can forgive you. I suggest if you haven't already, really begin reading His Word and praying.

Thank you, Natasha.

No problem. And maybe you can come to church with me sometime.

I'd love to, but I work on Sundays :(I'm a lifeguard.

It's cool, I go Wednesday nights also.

Great! In that case I can. Maybe I can bring my brother. I really want him to believe…He lost his faith. And maybe you can bring Natalia.

That would be awesome. I'll definitely ask her. Is your brother older or younger?

Older by two years. Man, I really hope he comes.

I hope so, too. But you'll see, the closer you get to God, He'll use you to draw your loved ones closer to Him. I'll pray for your brother. What's his name?

Bret.

I snatched my prayer notebook and pen off my headrest and jotted his name down.

Got it. He's officially added to the prayer list :)

Thank you. Really.

You're very welcome.

"Mamatutu," Mom called from downstairs, "can you help me set the table?"

"Yes, Mom."

I wrote back. *I have to go, I'm about to eat dinner. But we'll talk again soon. See you this Wednesday.*

All right. Have a goodnight. Dream sweet.

I smiled. *You too, Jonathan.*

***

The sun dazzled the foster home's little white chapel, tucked neatly toward the far right of the campus. A soft breeze whispered to the branches of the skinny trees sprinkled in front of it, casting lively shadows on the dusted ground. I looked at my phone: Wednesday, March 4th, 4:30pm. It rang suddenly, Jonathan's name appearing on the screen.

A smile made its way onto my mouth at the sight of my new friend's name. "Hello?"

"Hey, Natasha. What are you up to?"

"I'm over here at His House, a foster care home I volunteer at. I just got out so I'm waiting for my dad to pick me up."

"That's awesome."

"It really is. I love kids and these kids especially need to be loved. What are you up to?"

"Just at my dad's house." He paused. "Bret isn't coming tonight."

I sat on one of the chapel steps. "Don't worry, God will get him. Just keep praying. Natalia isn't coming either actually. She went to Tampa with the actors and director of her show." I kicked my feet against the dirt. "I don't know if you still wanna go…"

"No, I do. I just need your address."

"Oh, okay. I'll text it to you."

"Great. What time should I be at your house?"

"Service starts at 7:00, and it's in Fort Lauderdale, so I guess 6:15."

"All right, I'll see you then."

I smiled again as I said goodbye. The breeze disturbing the leaves retreated. Although Bret and Nati aren't coming, I think it's great that Jonathan still is. I know he's going to really like my church, but then again, non-denominational services are very different from Catholic ones. Sometimes people aren't used to change so they're afraid of it. Gosh, I hope the contrast doesn't scare him off…

Dad's burgundy Intrepid pulled up in front of the chapel, ruffling the dust out of

its slumber. I slipped my phone in my pocket as I approached the car. I guess I'll find out tonight if he plans on ever joining me again.

***

New Text Message: Jonathan.

Okay, can you maybe make a bonfire so I can find your house?

I chuckled as I walked into my kitchen. I'd get lost too if I was coming from west Pembroke Pines.

Lol, where are you now?

I'm passing a BP connect.

You're going the right way. Just make a left at the next light and my house is on that first street.

All right, see you soon.

I grabbed my Bible off the island and looked into the living room mirror. In a forest green long-sleeve that wrapped around my thumb, brown leggings, and brown boots, I looked like an elf. But elves rock so whatever. Thankfully, my curls are in tact, and my makeup is—wait a minute. Calm down, Natasha. You're almost acting like this is a date when it isn't. You hardly even know this boy.

I walked away from my reflection and peeked out the window. A silver 2000 Honda

Civic parked in the grass by the sidewalk. I bustled to the door, and then stopped. Should I be doing this? I really don't know Jonathan very well, yet I'm going in a car alone with him. I shrugged and then opened it.

Seated profile, Jonathan wore a purple button down, sleeves rolled up to his elbows. He fiddled with his nearly black hair, which shaded his eyes, as I drew closer to the car. I stifled a laugh as I knocked on the passenger side window. He recoiled, tossing a small plastic container into a cup-holder before reaching over and opening the door for me.

I let out some of my laugh as I glanced at the container of wax. I guess he wanted to look presentable as well.

"Sorry about that." Jonathan peered at me.

That odd flicker I've felt before sparked in my chest, which now encased a stuttering heart.

His eyes—almost identical to mine, just a tad greener and lighter—glimmered in the sunlight, a marvelous contrast to his dark hair and sun-kissed complexion. His nose sloped perfectly above his plump lips, smooth and free of lines.

He's the most gorgeous guy I've ever seen.

"Uh, it's okay," I answered a moment late.

Jonathan started the car and gripped the wheel as neared the stop-sign at the corner of my house. He rolled by without stopping while another car made a right turn. I leaned back in my chair as he hit the brakes, barely missing it.

He glanced at me. "We're not going to die, I promise."

"No worries, I trust you." I chuckled as I eased back into a normal sitting position. "So, this is your first time going to a nondenominational church, right?"

"Yeah. I go to a Catholic church."

"I used to be Catholic. Well, my parents weren't full-blown Catholic. We'd go to church sometimes, and I got baptized when I was eight, but I never got confirmed or anything. Then, when I was twelve or so, my uncle invited us to a Baptist church and it was the first time I understood why Jesus died for me. I realized that I had messed up, and he paid the price for it. That day my whole family walked up to the altar and said a prayer accepting Him into our heart. Then my mom's friend invited her to a non-denominational church and my dad's been going ever since, and I finally started going back six months ago."

Jonathan kept his stare rapt on the road. "That's really good. I'm the only one in my family who still goes to church every Sunday night when I get out of work. My mom said that even when I was a little kid, she'd walk in my room and find me praying. She said I would pray a lot, even for other people."

I smiled. *That's really sweet. I can't recall praying for anyone when I was a litt—*

He glimpsed at me, the setting sun shining on him, making the green in his eyes pop even more. *Gosh, I can barely keep my gaze off of him. Is it wrong to stare?*

His shoulders seemed tense. I quickly peered out the window. *Yeah, maybe I shouldn't be staring.*

We got off the exit leading to the church. *I don't consider this a date, but it is interesting meeting a guy for the first time and the place you go instead of a coffee shop or a movie is church. I can't think of a single rom-com where that happens. Then again, do Christian rom-coms even exist?*

"This is a church?" Jonathan said as we pulled up to the West side parking lot.

"Yes, but there's also a school here. And a restaurant. And a radio station. And a skate park."

He opened the car door for me. "Any maps?"

"Welcome." I stepped out and curtsied. "I'm Natasha, and will be your guide today."

Jonathan offered his arm. "I'm sure the tour is great, but…I think you're the main attraction."

Heat emerged from just about everywhere as I took his arm and led him to the main entrance. I'm flattered, but I hope he thinks otherwise after service…

A woman in a yellow dress greeted us with a warm smile and a mapless newsletter.

Jonathan surveyed the vast warehouse, his face unreadable. Oh, Lord, please don't let him be uncomfortable.

The band walked onto the stage and everyone rose as we entered a center row. The medium-tempo, perfectly orchestrated music saturated the space, and I forgot about everything as I sang along to the familiar song.

***

"So how did you like service?" I said to Jonathan as we walked out of the sanctuary.

His eyes avoided mine as we traversed outside into the early evening. "It was nice."

Just nice? Maybe he really was uncomfortable. I know how different

Catholic Mass is…maybe this wasn't a good idea?

A chill nipped through my thin long-sleeve. I rubbed my arms, and Jonathan suddenly slipped one of his around me. My heart responded with a leap. Those mesmerizing clear, green eyes swallowed my attention. All the passersby, the Christian music flowing from the restaurant's open doors, the children playing on the playground, it all vanished in his gaze.

Goodness, Natalia was actually right about a guy's appearance for once. Jonathan is extremely beautiful. But underneath his outer beauty, there is something different about him…this quiet and wholesome humility, and clearly, a reverence for God. The kid kneeled upon arrival to our row in the sanctuary, and upon exiting it. And these same gorgeous eyes shimmered with a softness toward God, which perhaps is what's most attractive of all…

"Natasha," a familiar voice said from behind.

You've gotta be kidding me. My stomach tumbled as I turned around. "Hey, Jax."

In a handsome gray suit, his brown hair neatly cut, Jax's smile faded as his eyes landed on Jonathan—still holding me.

I performed calm, cool, and collected. "Jax, this is Jonathan, a friend of my sister's." And Jonathan, this is Jax, also an old friend of my sister's who I kinda-sorta dated a few weeks back…

"Nice to meet you." Jonathan released me to shake Jax's hand.

Jax's eyebrow flinched. "You got a strong grip there."

Jonathan smiled so dang brilliantly. "Yeah."

I gestured to Jax's suit. "Look at you all businesslike."

He gave me one of his blushing smiles that I used to find cute. "I work for this Christian company now, helping people whose homes are getting foreclosed."

"That's great."

"Yes ma'am." His smile widened and he looked at me as though Jonathan was not even there.

Jonathan's arm returned to its place on my shoulder. I glanced at him. Those eyes also peered at me as if Jax was now invisible. Okay, time to go.

"Well, we're gonna get going," I said all too quickly.

Jax's smile dimmed. "All right, it was nice seeing you." He stepped forward and hugged me, holding on for a moment too long. "Keep in touch."

I offered a very small and civil smile as I pulled away. "Goodnight, Jax."

"Take care." Jonathan wrapped his arm around me again.

Jax's smile vanished. "You, too."

My cheeks flared with heat as me and Jonathan strode through the parking lot. How embarrassing. The last time I hung out with Jax we were supposed to become boyfriend and girlfriend. At least, in Jax's mind we were.

"Is he a friend of yours?" Jonathan said as we reached his car.

I continued the calm, cool, and collected act as I divulged. "He used to hang out with my sister when I was in sixth grade. I had a crush on him, but he wasn't a very innocent thirteen-year-old, so my sister forbade him from ever trying anything with me. Then I ran into him at the mall a couple of months ago and we exchanged numbers. He wanted to catch a movie, but I invited him to church instead and he ended up coming with his mom and sisters and they all walked up and he's been coming ever since." I hesitated as we reached the car. "We eventually ended up dating for maybe a month, and were supposed to make things official, but I didn't really like him so it didn't work out."

"Yeah…I kinda saw that whole story by the look in his eyes." Jonathan's mouth curved up as if he knew the epilogue somehow, and opened the passenger door for me. "So, where do you work?"

Glad that's over. My entire body relaxed as I stepped into his cozy Honda. "I teach musical theatre and drama to kids at a dance school."

"That sounds awesome."

"Yeah, I love it."

Jonathan hopped in and glanced at me as we drove away. "Do you work tomorrow?"

"Yeah."

"What do you usually eat for lunch?"

"Um, I don't know, anything. Why?"

"Because I wanna bring you lunch."

Warmth simmered in my neck. "I—no, it's okay, you don't have to."

"But I want to." Jonathan blessed me with his beautiful attention, so wholesome and yet so hot at the same time. "What's your favorite milkshake?"

Now that strange spark somehow designated for Jonathan before ever even meeting him in person, lit up my heart again, making it singe. "Strawberry banana."

"Okay. And you don't really know what you'd like for lunch…so how about…pizza?"

"Okay."

"What kind do you like?"

"Hawaiian."

That stunning Colgate smile brightened the whole car. "All right."

I turned my face toward the window to hide my smile—though I doubt it worked. No guy has ever brought me lunch before. I'm not really used to receiving anything from guys period. I mean, Dace had given me $100 and a pewter knife, but aside from that, I'd remained significantly ungifted. There was that other time when Red-Head-Ryan gave me a dozen long stem roses in the middle of the mall.

I wanted to crawl into a shell, it was super embarrassing, like a Hallmark movie gone wrong because Red-Head-Ryan was not at all on my radar as a potential love interest and it spurred his supposed best friend Elias, who I also didn't like at the time, to get me flowers the same night and deliver them before yet another full audience of mall-goers. Hopefully Jonathan doesn't make a scene. It's way worse in front of people you know and have to see several times a week. Including an ex who was supposed to let me know if we were getting back together again or not...I shifted in my seat. I totally forgot about that.

"What time do you get out?" Jonathan's sweet, sultry voice kindly disrupted.

"Class starts at four," I replied, "and ends at 5:30."

"5:30 it is then."

Words tumbled out of my mouth. "Would you like to watch me teach?"

Jonathan smiled, his beautiful eyes luminous even in the dark of the night. "Sure, but I can't make all of it because I get out of acting class at four."

"It's okay." I smiled back and then peered at the cars passing by on the highway. He's just a friend, Natasha. He's a nice guy —a nice gorgeous guy—but just a friend. A friend who wants to bring you lunch at work. Where you invited him to visit. Where your ex still teaches acro. And will be around at the same time. But again, it's all good because he hasn't texted for days, and you're focusing on Jesus. Not on relationships.

"So you and Natalia are in acting two together, right?" I asked.

"Yeah, she's a really good actress."

"She is. I'm excited that she got her first leading role."

"I know, it's awesome. She convinced me to audition for it, but I think I was too American. I couldn't fake a Cuban accent to save my life."

I laughed as he explained he was Italian and Peruvian, but born in Connecticut. And how he took acting class, but really preferred being behind the camera, though to me, he totally looked like he belonged in front of it.

We pulled up to my house where Natalia's lava-orange Mazda sat in the driveway.

Car still running, Jonathan turned his beautiful frame my way. "Thank you for inviting me to church."

"No problem at all." There has to be a way that I can get this guy to stay longer. I looked at Nati's car. "Would you like to come inside? Natalia's home."

Jonathan broke into one of his bright beams. "Sure."

I tried not to beam back as we got out and walked to my porch. I know I just met him, but I wanna spend more time with him, get to know him better, and though I adore my church, sitting and listening to a pastor teach doesn't allow for intimate conversation.

My front door opened the moment we reached the porch.

Natalia stood in a baggy t-shirt and Betty Boop pajama pants. "Well, well, well, what do we have here?" She giggled her mischievous, high-pitched Tales of the Crypt laugh that she used to terrorize me with as a kid. "Come on inside, lovebirds."

I shot lasers at her with my eyes as we stepped into the living room. Dang it, Nati, please don't embarrass me for once.

Jonathan ambled in, all pleasant and perhaps pleased with her assessment…I mean she did say that he said I was too beautiful for him. Hopefully he still carried the same view after seeing me in person…

"What's up, Natalia?"

Nati leaned on the island. "You tell me, Sappy. Taking out my little sister now?"

"Not really. We went to church."

"Hi, Mamatu." Mom emerged from the Florida room, also in her handy-dandy t-shirt dress jammies. She hugged me and then turned to Jonathan, wide-eyed. "Who's this?"

"This is my theatre friend, Jonathan," Natalia said as if she'd just won an Oscar.

"Oh, I saw your pictures. You look different in person."

My eyes bulged. Oh man, Natalia and Mom together equals embarrassment squared!

Jonathan smiled politely. "Yeah, they're pretty old."

Nati glided into a chair by the island like a skulking snake. "So, how was church? Did you like it? My sister's been trying to get me to go. I used to go sort of when I was like sixteen."

"Yeah, it was great. You should've gone." He looked at me, his complexion gold in the warm lighting of the kitchen, making him look all the dreamier.

"I was in Tampa with the cast doing research for the show."

His beautiful eyes still watched me. "Maybe next time."

"I need to take the trash out," Mom announced.

"I'll take it for you." Jonathan's gaze finally left mine as he walked to the trash bin and removed the bag.

"Aww, thank you," Mom said, as if she hadn't planned for him to do the chore for her.

"I'll go with you." Natalia hopped out of the chair. "You may need some protection. We do live in the hood you know." She jiggled her eyebrows at me as she led him out.

Jonathan looked at me one last time before closing the door behind him. I nearly melted into the island.

Mom hunched over the counter. "You guys are like, mesmerized by each other."

I glanced at the door. Me mesmerized by Jonathan? Maybe a little. But him mesmerized by me? I kind of like that idea. Not too much, like in an obsessive Edward-Bella kind of way, but in a somewhat fascinated way is totally fine.

It wasn't long before Natalia and Jonathan walked back inside, although I know it would've been shorter if Jonathan went alone. God only knows what she was saying to him out there. Well whatever it was, it must have been good, because he's illuminating the room with his gorgeous smile. Man…great hair, beautiful eyes, perfect nose, good skin, a radiant smile that makes him look like he's in a Colgate commercial. What girl wouldn't look twice at him when he walks into a room? Those alluring hazel eyes met mine again, demanding I ignore everyone else.

"So, Sappy, you're going to the play still, right?" Nati asked Jonathan.

"I wouldn't miss it for anything."

That spark that poked me after seeing Natalia had texted him back in my stead returned.

Jonathan laughed. "Your audition was epic."

Natalia soaked in the flattery, bowing low. "Oh, please. You so would've landed the role as my husband if you only knew how to fake an accent."

"It's pretty lame that my Gringo accent was the only thing holding Moriah back from casting me."

"But hey, Short Ribs is coming up and you've got that epic romance scene with Cynthia."

Jonathan let out another cute laugh. "I can't wait to perform that one. Cynthia is super talented."

As Nati and him continued in their mutual-acting-class-insider-convo, I excused myself to the Florida room, that annoying spark pestering. A romance scene with Cynthia? Whatever, Jonathan is just a friend anyway. Let him catch up with Nati. It's not like they have classes together twice a week.

As they shared more laughs, I plopped onto the couch and turned up the volume on the Tyra Banks Show. I focused hard on the lovely ex-model as she strutted about in a "fat suit" to experience what it felt like being obese. The laughing continued, as did my seething. I inhaled sharply and slapped the floor with my elvish boot. After a few minutes, Natalia finally announced she was going to get some beauty sleep and departed to her new living quarters. Mom declared the same after telling Jonathan he can stay and watch TV with me.

He sauntered into the Florida room and sat beside me. "What are you watching." A slight caution colored his tone. So he finally picked up on the fact that I found it a tad annoying that he chose to blow ten minutes of our precious time conversing with my big, drop-dead-gorgeous sister.

Still playing it cool, I glimpsed at him. "Do you wanna watch this?"

"I don't mind."

A smile betrayed my feelings as I focused on the screen. He seems so easygoing. And although he's ridiculously handsome, it's effortless being around him. I feel so comfortable, like I've known him for years.

A jolt of boldness took over. I laid my hand atop his and he twined his fingers with mine. I settled more into the couch as a sense of peace rested on my heart. I know I've thought this before and been so terribly wrong, but this really feels right.

I tightened my grip as we continued to watch, hours passing as we sat in silence, enjoying each other's presence.

6. MOVING ON

| practically skipped into the studio office to pick up my check while my students drank water from the fountain. Thoughts about last night with Jonathan saturated my mind; how he'd stared at me with those dreamy hazel eyes, and smile at me with that gorgeous Colgate mouth. Our innocent non-date was just perfect—minus the brief Natalia intermission.

Fake-smiling-Stacey dawdled over a planner at the desk. Her hair-sprayed curls sat on either side of her head as stiffly as she did. "Hi, Natasha."

"Hi, Stacey!"

She removed my check from the drawer and handed it to me, her eyebrow raised as if I was some looney she wasn't sure she should give it to.

"Thanks, Stacey!" I grinned as I turned to leave. She has no id—I halted, my heart clobbering my chest as Dace stared at me, his eyes darker than usual. "Sorry," I said as he stepped around me and strode into the office as if I were a random piece of furniture. "Uh, bye, Dace."

I squinted at him as he grabbed his check and walked past me again and exited the studio without so much as a glimpse my way. What is with him? Just a few days ago he had a talk with Marilyn about leaving August for good and trying again with me, and we were texting each other, too, here and there.

I rolled my eyes as I scurried into the hallway. "Come on, guys."

My students followed me outside to studio four as Dace hopped into his run-down Altima and sped off like something out of a Fast and Furious movie. Well, at least I don't have to worry about him and Jonathan running into each other today.

I bustled into the studio. "All right, kiddies, you did a great job today. I'm super excited for the show. Practice the dance steps at home in front of the mirror, okay?"

"Yes, Ms. Natasha," they replied in unison like the adorable ensemble they were.

"Thank you." I smiled at the little cutie-pies. "Now get out of here!"

Victoria and Skyler gave me a hug before trotting out of the room. A butterfly fluttered in my stomach. Jonathan stood in the doorway, wearing his flawless smile, a pizza box in one hand and a milkshake in the other. I beamed as I approached him.

"Sorry I'm so late," he said, a super pleasant aroma emerging from his presence —and it was not the pizza. "It was kind of a mission to get this stuff."

I blushed. He went through a mission just to get lunch for me?

"I hope you like Anthony's," he continued. "I heard they're one of the best pizza places." He gave me the box and milkshake. "I'm also sorry if it's cold. There wasn't a Steak-n-Shake anywhere near the Anthony's so I got the shake in Pembroke Pines."

"Pembroke Pines? There's a Steak-n-Shake a few miles down on Biscayne."

"Oh." He gave me his humble and hot smile. "I'm not very familiar with this area, but it's okay though, because it was for you."

My face grew hotter. "So, where should we go to eat this?"

Jonathan stood at my side as we strolled out. "Wherever you want."

I pondered for a moment. Where is a quiet, public place, with not too many people? "The beach?"

"Sure, just tell me where to go."

"Okay." I followed him to his car, my blushing beginning to give me heat flashes.

I'm so not good at being treated this way from a guy, especially a super hunky one that I'm really starting to like. "Thanks so much for doing all this," I said as he opened the passenger door for me.

"It's not a problem. I'm glad I was able to bring you lunch."

"No guy has ever done that for me before."

"That's strange." He walked around to the driver's side and got in. "I would think tons of guys would be offering to bring you lunch."

"Nope, just you."

Those sea-green, dusted with sand irises shimmered like the sun was made to shine off them. "I'm glad I can be your first."

And I hope you'll be the last… "So how far exactly is west Pembroke Pines from my job?"

"About forty minutes."

"Forty minutes?"

"Yeah." He smirked as I gaped at him.

Okay, I think it's safe to say he may be starting to like me, too. *God said He's going to make it clear for you very soon.* The words Prophet Martin spoke to me at that event five days ago replayed in my mind. It is strange that the day after I go to church with Jonathan, Dace suddenly stops talking to me.

And there's no way he knows about Jonathan. And when he spoke to Marilyn, she said he was really going to consider breaking off all ties with August and starting over with me. So why is he suddenly ignoring me?

Finally, one day my ex went from, 'I love you,' to, 'I want nothing to do with you.' And I mean out of nowhere, and I knew it was God hardening his heart against me. Kelly's voice played in my head now. That makes perfect sense! Maybe God is hardening Dace's heart so I can really move on…to Jonathan.

I glimpsed at him. Okay, don't jump too far ahead and get your hopes up just to have them crash to the ground later if nothing becomes of this. Been there, done that, and I don't plan on visiting the Heartbreak Hotel again anytime soon.

The New Port Beach entrance appeared out the window.

"Turn right here!" I said.

Jonathan slammed on the brakes, jolting us both forward. "I'm sorry."

"It's okay."

I surveyed him as he turned into the parking lot, making sure he really was okay with my potentially fatal absentmindedness. He didn't seem perturbed in the slightest. All right, maybe I should save the contemplative thoughts for times when I'm not navigating.

We got out of the car and strolled toward the sand, the beach just how I assumed it would be: quiet and desolate—minus the flock of seagulls passing through.

Oh no.

The seagulls stared at the box of pizza in my hands. The ones on the ground rapid-hobbled toward us while the ones in the air swarmed menacingly.

"Come on!" Jonathan broke out into a run. I followed beside him as the seagulls trailed us. "Over here." He sprinted to a stack of lounge chairs a few yards ahead.

We stopped behind the chairs, ducking as the seagulls flew overhead and continued down the beach.

I panted. "I can't believe we almost got attacked by hungry birds."

"They must be bioengineered."

I laughed. "Like a flock straight out of Resident Evil."

"Exactly." Jonathan donned an intense tone, as if he was acting on a movie set and the scene called for it.

I mimicked his performance, eying the surroundings while slowly opening the box and then handed him a piece. He glanced around before taking it and joined in with my laughter, his chuckles soft and quiet. His laugh is sweet, like him.

He stared at me as our laughter died down. "You're really pretty."

I smiled at him. I would say he's really cute, but I don't think I should.

"Do you hear that?" Jonathan looked down the stretch of sand. Beyond the gentle rustle of waves, live music played in the distance.

"Is that fifties music?" I asked.

"Yeah, I think so."

"I love romantic songs from the fifties."

"Me, too. It's pretty much my goal in life to be a Greaser."

I tried to not be obvious as I observed him. He seems like he's from the fifties, so polite and respectful, even when he gives a compliment. Doesn't curse, doesn't drink. Am I dreaming, 'cause I think guys like him just don't exist. "I'd say you're not too far off, though you don't seem like the bad boy type…"

"I've had my moments."

"Oh?"

"But I've moved on."

"Good to know. I'm kinda over bad boys." I lay down and rested my head on his lap. "Wanna go to my best friend Marilyn's house after this? She has a really nice pool."

He smiled down on me, breeze blowing his hair back, all swooney. "Sure."

The wind picked up more as a slight drizzle fell from the darkening sky. So much for going in the pool.

"We should start heading out before it rains harder," Jonathan said.

"Good idea."

He helped me to my feet and we jogged back to the car as the rain increased. We made is to his car just as the downpour started. I dialed Marilyn.

"Hello?" She practically screamed in my ear.

I lowered the volume as I replied. "Hey, Mar. Can I come over with a friend?"

"A friend?"

"He's a friend of Natalia's from theatre class, but a friend of mine too, now."

"Oh, I see. Sure, why not?"

"Thanks. See you soon."

"I guess things didn't work out with Dace?"

"We'll talk later." I quickly hung up. Come on Mar, not while I'm right next to the guy and your super loud voice might be heard.

I directed Jonathan to her place, and in minutes we parked across her building. The rain still clobbered the car as Jonathan turned off the engine. I decided to take advantage of the forced proximity. "While we wait for the rain to stop, let's ask each other questions."

Jonathan's plump lips curled. "Okay."

"I'll start. What's your favorite color?"

"Green and purple."

"Oh my gosh, green's my favorite color and purple's my second."

"We have good taste." He smiled, his pearly white teeth gleaming despite the gray dreariness outside. His sharp incisors looked like…fangs! Oh my gosh. My heart sprinted. He's the guy from my dream!

The words cascaded from my mouth. "I had a dream about you!"

A crease lodged between his perfect, ebony eyebrows. "A dream?"

"Yeah, a few weeks ago, I had a dream that I was about to be attacked by a vampire and another vampire stepped in. And he had dark hair, not too short, not too long, like yours, and light eyes. And his face was just like yours."

Jonathan smiled again. "That is so cool…but slightly creepy."

"Yeah, you're not a vampire are you?"

"I do have these." He pointed at his teeth. "Alas, I am but a human."

I shook my head as I surveyed the dream boy. "That's so weird…"

What does this mean? I forced my mind elsewhere before I could start obsessing over signs and get myself all confused like I've done too often before. "Anyways, it's your turn."

Jonathan smirked. "What's your favorite vampire movie?"

"Blade, and From Dusk till Dawn."

He scrutinized me like a lawyer questioning a witness. "I love Blade, and Robert Rodriguez is my favorite director."

"Oh my gosh, that's so cool. After watching Blade Trinity I got inspired to write an action book about vampires. I only got to the sixth chapter though."

We continued our back-and-forth-game, and between writing, drawing, making home videos when we were kids, to our favorite love movie being *A Walk to Remember,* we were twins in the common interests department.

I looked out the windshield. The rain finally calmed. "Maybe we should continue this later. Marilyn's probably wondering where we are."

"Let's not disappoint her."

I gave my Mama-Bestie a call and she directed me to her pool. We found her sitting by the jacuzzi, face downcast as she dipped her feet into the water. As we drew near, her baby-blues widened.

Barely able to hold back a smile, I said as casually as I could, "Marilyn, this is Jonathan."

"Nice to meet you." Jonathan extended a hand.

She also purposed to keep it casual, but a blushing smile failed her. "So, how do you know each other? Natalia right?"

"Yeah." I slipped into the Jacuzzi. "He's in acting two with her."

"Oh…so how did you meet him?"

Jonathan gave her a quick run-down before dunking under the water.

"You guys went to church together?" Marilyn said as he came up.

"Yeah." He smiled before peering at me, the lights in the Jacuzzi making his eyes an extra light green. He looked almost surreal as the water from his black hair dripped down his face.

I don't know if it's the Jacuzzi or him, but I'm definitely getting light-headed. I turned to Mar and whispered in her ear before walking out of the Jacuzzi. "He's like a dream."

Mar pinched my arm. "You seem pretty awake to me."

I headed toward the pool. "It's really hot in there."

Marilyn and the dream boy followed. She sat on the edge as Jonathan and I stepped inside, her brow puckered as the sorrow returned to her eyes.

"Let me guess," I said. "Alex."

Jonathan swam closer to the edge. "Who's Alex?"

"Her wannabe boyfriend."

"What did he do?"

Mar's forehead crumpled. "The other day, his friend said something really rude to me right in front of him and he didn't even defend me."

My lioness growled from within. "This isn't the first time he's done something like that." I paddled next to Jonathan. "And they've been acting like they've been going out for months, but he hasn't made it official yet."

Marilyn watched the ripples I made, her eyes glistening.

"You both are so different, Mar. He doesn't treat you right and he's not for you."

"If a guy really likes you," Jonathan said, his tone tender, "he won't be afraid to ask you out. And about him not being right for you, I was on and off with my ex for six-

and-a-half months. I was day and she was night."

Mar and I exchanged a glance as he continued.

"We both messed up a lot. Sometimes, a wrong thing can't be made right."

Marilyn's pretty gaze lowered to the water, still sad, but now also pensive. Meanwhile, I tried to mask my emotions. It's too strange that he was with his ex for the same amount of time I was with Dace, and his choice of words, 'I was day and she was night.' That's exactly how it was with him and I. Me, 'the walking pile of love,' and Dace, the dark fighter who balked at the idea of loving God and others. The wrong that couldn't be made right…

Marilyn stretched. "I'm gonna go. I'm tired."

I climbed out of the pool and gave her a light hug.

"Thanks." She smiled faintly. "It was nice meeting you, Jonathan."

"You, too."

I sighed as she trudged away. She doesn't have to settle for the Alex's of this world. If she only knew how much God loves her, that the void in her heart she hopes Alex will fill can't be filled by him…

As I rejoined Jonathan in the water, Marilyn's words that night at the mall eased into my mind. *"Why are you upset? None of them are the one. The one is still coming. And he's going to blow them both out of the water."*

7. SEALING THE DEAL

"He's coming over again?" Mom gawked at me as I removed a jug of water from our kitchen fridge.

I grinned as I poured myself a cup. "Yes."

"Okay, this is the fourth day in a row since your little church outing that he comes to see you. What the heck did you do to him?"

"It's the third, Mom. And I don't know, we just...clicked."

Nancy Drew lifted a thin brow at me as I sat on a stool. This whole thing was definitely unexpected—a pleasant and quite incredulous surprise. Natalia had proven to be a terrible matchmaker in the past, but she somehow hit a bullseye with Jonathan. *I believe God wants you two to meet.* That made it the most odd of all. Natalia and God were more like acquaintances than anything else. Though—prayerfully—that'd change some day.

A few knocks rattled the front door. I scurried out of my seat.

"Wait! Desperation nation." Mom held me back, and then sauntered to the door like a turtle in chancletas. She gestured for me to sit back down before she opened it. "Hello, Jonathan."

"Hi, Mrs. Sanchez." Jonathan, today in a fitted green tee that matched his irises and black string necklaces, hugged her before turning to me. "Hi."

"Hi." I strode toward him, much to Mom's dismay I'm sure, and received his incredible embrace. Warmth showered over me. If there was a world's best hugger contest, I'm sure he'd win first place.

As we released, Nancy Drew cocked her blow-dried blonde head. "Why are you always wearing those little black strings around your neck?"

"Mom." I eyed her before turning to him. She can't find anything bad to point out about the guy so she decides to rag on his jewelry. "Wanna go outside and watch the stars?"

"Sure."

"Great." I poked her with my glare once more before trotting up the stairs and grabbing a blanket from the closet. I feel bad for whoever's going to be her son-in-law.

I swiftly returned to my handsome visitor and whisked him through the Florida room and outside, evading Mom before a full-blown investigation could take place. The moon shined full and bright, full of wonder and hope.

We sat together on the blanket and I couldn't stop myself from resting my head on Jonathan's warm shoulder. He's like something out of a fifties flick. Handsome, wholesome, and just flat out pleasant, we don't even have to talk and yet I have a good time.

I looked up at him. He pressed his smooth forehead against mine. My heartbeat hastened. *God, if it's okay for us to kiss, then let him kiss m*—Jonathan's soft lips touched mine, so tender and almost…respectful somehow.

That sense of peace cloaked me as I kissed him back. This feels so…right. I smiled as I slowly pulled away from him.

"What?" he asked.

"I prayed in my mind that if it was okay for you to kiss me for you to go for it, and you did."

A smile grew on his lips. "It's weird, earlier today I heard that song, 'This kiss' and right now it came into my mind out of nowhere, and I just…went for it."

I lay my head on his shoulder again. The way he kissed me was unlike any first kiss I've ever had—and I've had plenty since fourth grade. It didn't feel like pure lust. It was genuine care…

I peered up at the stars. *What are You up to?*

***

Cell phone in hand as I lay in bed listening to Christian music, I read Jonathan's latest text:

Listen to 'Earth Angel' by the Penguins. It reminds me of you.

I hopped off my bed and ran into Natalia's official bedroom. She sat in front of the computer in pajama pants, as is her custom. "Nati, YouTube 'Earth Angel.' Jonathan texted me saying to listen to it because it reminds him of me."

"Oh wow." She quickly obliged and an oldies piano tune strutted out of the speakers, a chorus of men singing, 'Oh' before one began a solo.

"Earth Angel, Earth Angel
Will you be mine?
My darling dear

Love you all the time
I'm just a fool
A fool in love with you…
I hope and I pray that someday
I'll be the vision of your hap-happiness."

I smacked my chest. "Awwww, he's so cute!"

Nati touched her lips. "I think I just vomited in my mouth."

I ignored her comment, swaying to the song until it finished and then hurriedly texted Jonathan back.

I listened to the song. I loved it :)

I sank onto Nati's twin-sized bed. What a lovely song. Quaint and fifties sounding, like him…Oh yeah, I have to go to work. "Nati, can you take me to Honey's?"

"When do you need to go?"

I smiled. "Now."

"Fine." She stretched as she stood up.

"Thanks, I love you!"

"Yeah, yeah."

Jonathan texted back as we got into Nati's lava-colored Mazda.

The vision of your happiness: that's how I feel about you. You're the vision of my happiness.

I sighed as we pulled out of the driveway. I just wanna be with him alre—oh no. It's too soon. You always rush in. But he's different. Maybe God's cool with this. Oh gosh. I clasped my forehead. Lord, I don't know if it's Your will…

"Dude, are you okay?" Natalia examined me like Mom would.

"Please, keep your eyes on the road." I wrote Jonathan back.

Jonathan, I really like you…

I slapped the phone onto my lap.

Nati glanced at me. "Yo, what is going on?"

"Okay, I really like Jonathan, but I don't know if it's too soon to become boyfriend and girlfriend."

"Oh." Nati fixed her stare ahead. "Well, if you're confused, just wait."

Hmm. That makes sense. But I kind of do wanna go out with him…

My phone chimed.

I really like you, too. I wouldn't mind being more than your friend.

My heart banged against my chest like a drum as I texted back.

If you mean what you said, I want to be yours, but I don't know. Should we wait?

I don't know. I mean, I like you a lot, Natasha, but I don't want to make you feel rushed.

I really like him a lot, too. And he's so different from every guy I've ever been with, every guy I've ever met.

I think we should pray for an answer or something. Like this feels right, but I want to make sure it's what He wants.

I put the phone down and bowed my head. God, do you want me and Jonathan to become boyfriend and girlfriend? Can you please reveal it to us?

Okay, I just prayed.

I did, too. I mean, in a way we're acting like we are going out.

He's got a point…

Okay. I think it's okay if we embrace the 'title' but we have to make sure the spiritual side of our relationship comes first. Like, I wanna help you get closer to God, not draw you away from Him.

You won't.

I smiled as I punched the keypad. As long as he understands God's number one, that's good enough for me.

Okay. Next time I see you, if you'll have me, I'm your's.

Okay :D

All right then. It's settled. Now all we need to do is seal it with a kiss.

***

Why isn't anyone answering the phone? From my seat in Honey's lobby, I glanced up from my cell at Stacey, seated at the studio's front desk fiddling with office materials, pretending to be busy. Poor thing probably can't wait to go home, and here she is—7:30 at night—stuck waiting for someone to pick me up.

Jonathan.

Right! But he lives like thirty-five minutes away...I shrugged and shot him a text.

Hey, Jonathan. I'm kind of stuck at Honey's. No one's answering my calls.

May I come to your rescue?

I beamed. Gosh this boy's gotta knack with words.

Yes please :)

A quiver rippled across my chest. Oh my gosh, that means I'm going to see him tonight. The last time we spoke we determined we'd make things official. Tonight I might become Jonathan's girlfriend!

"Did you find someone to pick you up, honey?" Stacey examined me from her perch.

I kept my face even, although my heart bounded within. "Yes, ma'am. He's on his way now."

"Oh, how good." She went back to organizing the desk. If I didn't know any better, I'd say she rolled her eyes just before her fluffy curls covered hid them.

"I'm gonna wait outside." I walked out of the studio and sat on a curb beneath the starry sky. Jonathan and I have known each other for about six days now. Yeah...that is definitely a short amount of time. But for some reason, it feels like I've known him longer. And I mean, where in the Bible is there a rule about how long you should date someone before going steady with him anyway? As far as I'm concerned, there isn't one. And didn't Jacob kiss Rachel the same night he met her? And then told her dad he'd work seven years so he can take her as his wife. He only knew her for a day, but that's all he needed to prove he wanted to spend the rest of his life with her.

The silver Honda pulled into a parking space across from me. More adrenaline coursed through my veins as Jonathan got out of the car. Spunky, black leather jacket on, a skip in his step, and looking like the lead in a new Outsiders movie, he neared. He stopped in the pool of light I now also stood in, his hazel eyes shimmering. "Hi, earth angel."

I purposed not to swoon like a fangirl. "Hi, dream boy."

Stacey scrambled out of the studio and then halted. "Oh, he's here."

"Yes, ma'am," I said. "Jonathan, this is Stacey."

"Nice to meet you." Jonathan took her hand.

"You, too." She shook his hand briskly, her cheeks shifting to pink—despite the fact that she's old enough to be his mom. "Goodnight."

I stifled a laugh as she hurried away. "Thanks again for waiting with me!"

"No problem!" She called without looking back.

Jonathan offered his perfect smile. "Shall we?"

My hands shook as he accompanied me to the car. This might be it: the night Jonathan becomes my boyfriend. But what if he changed his mind on his way over here? I mean it was a nearly forty-minute drive. Maybe he thought about the fact that it's only been six days that we've known each other, and didn't end up with the same conclusion I did…

Maybe this whole thing is one massively bad idea. Frustratingly, I'm pretty notorious for impulsive, recklessly stupid choices in the romance department. Just because I love Jesus now doesn't mean I've got this particular area down pact yet. Maybe I should wait? Or run a thousand miles in the opposite direction.

It seemed as though only minutes passed and we were parking in front of my house.

Jonathan's gaze met mine.

I held my breath. Why isn't he turning off the car? Am I right? Did he really reconsider asking me out?

"I'll walk you to the door." He shut off the ignition.

I struggled to control my shakes as we walked to my porch. All right, maybe this is a good thing—or maybe not. I've had doom walks to this very porch a number of times. The last one a final goodbye to a relationship...

My quivers worsened as we reached my doorstep. Control yourself, Natasha. If he doesn't ask you out, it's not the end of the world. It just means it's too soon, or he's... not the one.

Jonathan's dreamy eyes locked me in place. Okay, maybe it won't be the end of the world, but I might just cry over it for a night or two.

He suddenly knelt down on one knee. "Natasha, can I have the honor of having you as my girlfriend?"

Heat trickled into my cheeks as I giggled, relieved and embarrassed at his knightly display and my fidgety second-guessing. "Yes."

As Jonathan stood, he slipped his hand onto my waist. And then, the kiss came. My trembling subsided as he kissed me gently, like I was a delicate flower he was afraid of damaging. The deal is sealed. Jonathan Sapienza is officially my boyfriend.

8. Meet My Ex

Trying to focus on teaching after the amazingness of last night is quite a task.

"Okay kids: five, six, seven, eight." Standing by the stereo in my stretchy dress and leggings, I hit the play button. Seussical's 'The biggest blame fool' number boomed throughout studio four. The students began the dance I taught them last week. I totally feel like dancing along with them. Just less than three weeks ago my heart was shattered to pieces over ending things with Dace. Then a week ago I meet Jonathan, and now I'm his girlfriend. It's almost unbelievable.

The kids moved off beat, some of them way off. I restarted the song. Okay, I really need to try and pay more atten—Jonathan stood in the doorway. Wearing a black 'Love me' shirt, a gorgeous smile lit up his exquisite face. So much for paying attention.

I walked backward toward the doorway. "Keep practicing the steps without the music, and follow Shelly's lead."

My students giggled and whispered as I faced Jonathan. He met me halfway, one of his hands behind his back.

"What are you doing here?" I asked. "I thought you were gonna—"

He slowly brought his hand around, revealing a huge bouquet of two-dozen, long-stem, red roses.

"Oh my gosh!" My cheeks blazed as Skyler and the other bird girl 'oohed' and clapped. I took the stunning flowers. "Why did you bring these?"

His lips curved up. "Just because."

I shook my head. Just because? Is this boy for real? I peered up at the clock. 5:35.

I spun toward my students. "All right guys, see you tomorrow. This number is coming out great!"

As they filed out of the room—still giggling and whispering—I threw my arms around Jonathan. I closed my eyes as he held me. Everything about him is so...refreshing.

Some little girls from another class stared at us through the window, snickering like Jonathan was their favorite pop star.

I quickly released him. "So are we going to visit my grandma in the hospital?"

"Yes we are."

"Okay." I scuttled to the door, trying to hide the roses, but failing. "Is it me, or is every girl in this studio staring at you?"

A little brunette in a glittery tutu I've seen in acro held her cell phone up, facing Jonathan. She stared at the screen, squealed, and then ran away.

"Oh my, did she really just take a picture of you? You'd think you were a Jonas brother the way these little girls are acting."

He smirked. "Are you jealous?"

"Actually, I'm flattered that my boyfriend is striking to young and old alike."

He laughed his quiet chuckle, his beautiful teeth glistening whiter than the walls. It's so awesome that I can call him that now. As we turned the corner my heart missed a beat.

Dace's dark eyes locked onto us as he leaned on the counter of the front desk, his laughter with Christine, the volunteer receptionist who I always knew had a crush on him, coming to an end.

Christine shifted her focus from him, her sharp brown eyes now on Jonathan. "Natasha, is this the 'dream boy' you were telling me about?"

Dace looked away.

"Yeah. Jonathan, this is Christine."

"Pleasure to meet you," he said.

Dace glanced at me, the first time he'd showed me any attention at all since his random ignoring stint. I quickly redirected my focus, a strange sense of darkness beginning to fester.

My sight met Jonathan. "I'm gonna get my check really quick."

"Okay."

I whizzed into the office. Jonathan's never seen Dace, but I did tell him he works with me. Maybe he can sense that's him. Dang it—and I left him out there alone with him! And with Christine, who's not helping the situation very much.

I grabbed my check from the desk drawer and scurried back to Jonathan's side. "Got it."

"He's so Twilight," Christine purred, as if my boyfriend wasn't standing in the same room as her. "He reminds me of Edward."

"Well we have to go, bye, Christine," I said maybe too swiftly, that awkward darkness still emanating from Dace.

"Okay. It was nice meeting you, Edward," Christine said yet again.

I grabbed Jonathan's hand. "He's better than Edward." We veered around, our steps perfectly synchronized, leaving the awkwardness—and the darkness—behind us. As the golden hour melted into place and we reached his car, I confessed, "That was my ex."

"I think I made a good impression." Jonathan opened the passenger door for me.

I surveyed him as he got inside. He really doesn't seem to mind. Well, if he's fine then I should just let it go. The last thing I need is a conversation about Dace to mess things up with Jonathan and I.

He held my hand as we drove away from the studio. Yeah, the past is over and done with. That chapter of my life is finished. From now on, I won't bring up Dace anymore.

***

"You really didn't have to take me here." I took another countless bite of savory, fondue steak, compliments of the glorious Melting Pot—and Jonathan.

Sitting beside me in the burgundy booth with its own pewter, privacy curtains, Jonathan glowed like a nineteen-year-old dream boat from a fifties flick. "I really did."

Face warming up again for the millionth time—and not from the steaming pot on the table—I put my fork down and studied this walking dream. His eyes seemed to melt when they looked into mine. A reflection perhaps of what I felt every time I gazed at him. I feel like those girls in Beauty and the Beast that fawn over Gaston, but I can't help it. Lightheaded, I shut out the beautiful vision before me and chose instead to rest my head on his shoulder.

That Shulamite woman in the Song of Songs mentioned feeling weak with love and needing a raisin cake.

Oh my gosh. An overwhelming sensation permeated my heart. No—it's too soon. You've only known each other for nine days. But he's so…right for me.

"Jonathan…" I said quietly. "I…love you."

Why and how it happened after nine days, I don't know, but it's true. I do…

Jonathan's voice met my ear. "I love you, too, Natasha."

Heart definitely charged up, I pulled back enough to see his lovely face.

He leaned into me and pressed his mouth to mine. My heartbeat slowed with every sweet moment. I can't believe all this. Jonathan and I, after such a short time, have fallen in love. Could he be…the one?

I pulled away, gasping for air.

Jonathan frowned at me. "Are you okay?"

"Yeah, I just forgot to breathe."

He brushed a strand of hair away from my face as he smiled. "I asked God whoever the one was, to have her say I love you first."

"You did? But why?"

"I don't know really. I also hoped she'd be blonde." He paused. "And a virgin."

I tilted my head. Wait, how does he— Natalia! She always offers that information about me. I remember even hearing her do it on a few occasions: *And this is my little sister. She's a really good girl, she's still a virgin.* Ugh, whatever, it's not like I'm ashamed of it. But I'm curious as to why that matters to Jonathan.

I surveyed him. "Why did you want her to have those qualities?"

"Well, my ex was a brunette so I wanted someone different. And I wanted a virgin because I had an issue with trust. When I was with a girl, and I knew she had sex before me, I would feel differently toward her. I know it sounds messed up because I wasn't a virgin myself, but it just really bothered me for some reason. I guess you can say it was a forgiveness issue."

I picked up my fork again to garner more strength for this conversation. "I can understand that. There's this book, 'For Young Women Only,' and it has all these surveys of different questions asked to a variety of young men on the topic of girls, and one of the surveys said that over eighty percent of guys wanted to marry a virgin. And there was one quote where a guy said that after him and his girlfriend started having sex he became confused about his love for her. He didn't know if he loved her for her, or for how she made him feel. He said he missed the innocence of just cuddling."

Jonathan nodded as his eyes gleamed. "Yeah, I regretted having sex. I had two partners and then my ex, but with her especially was when I started to feel bad about it. It's like, I knew God didn't want me having sex before marriage, but I tried to make excuses. I would even fall to my knees and apologize, but I'd still do it." He looked at the table before raising his gaze again, his face resolute. "After my ex and I broke up, I really wanted to commit to being abstinent. Now that I'm with someone who wants to be pure till marriage, I can stay true to that commitment."

I held his hand. "We should get purity rings."

"Purity rings?"

Another heat wave slapped my face. Maybe I shouldn't have mentioned the word, 'rings' right after exchanging thee three words. I forked another piece of meat. "Yeah, they usually have 'true love waits' engraved on them."

Jonathan dipped some cheese in the pot, his face all resolute again. "I think it's important."

I laid my head against his chest as our waiter returned with our dessert. It's unbelievable I have a guy who's willing to respect me by waiting until—marriage? Hmm…marry Jonathan someday?

I pulled away from him, my cheeks hurting from all the smiling he's caused today. Yeah, I don't think I'd mind. I don't think I'd mind at all.

9. THE CROSSFIRE

Why am I doing this?

The darkness in Natalia's room began to exude life as I continued to read the words on the computer screen.

> *This darkness, it rises inside*
> *It fuels my fire*
> *Consumes my insight*
> *Controls my every desire…*
> *No escaping the affliction*
> *No light in the gloom*
> *No hope for a sunrise*
> *This black heart entombs.*

Tears filled my eyes. The date of this post from Dace was two days ago was March 19th, on Nati's birthday. I feel so bad. Can't he see there's hope for him? He doesn't have to accept darkness and emptiness—no matter how messed up the situation, there's always hope because God doesn't shy away from darkness. If invited, He enters into the midst of it and completely extinguishes it. I know. Firsthand.

I opened my photos folder and scanned through them until I found one of us—the last one we took together at the restaurant, where his smile was so joyful—then returned to his Facebook and wrote him a message.

Dace,

There can always be light, no matter how dark the situation. Please don't give up. I haven't given up on you. There's always hope. Please remember that. I love you. But most importantly, God loves you.
-Natasha

I copied the picture and pasted it to the bottom of the message and hit send. From now on, I'll pray even harder for him. I believe with prayer, he'll make it through someday.

I wiped my eyes as I walked out of the dark room and into my own. Please help him, God. He walked with You once, he's just walked away. But chase him down. Please. Help him find the light he used to have.

My phone rang from my headrest.

I grabbed it: *My Dream Boy.*

I smiled as I sat on my bed—despite the sadness for my ex's still messed up condition weighing on my heart. "Hey, handsome."

"Hey, what are you doing now?"

"I just got off the computer. Now I'm in my room."

"Did you message Dace?"

My heartbeat quickened. Oh no. Dace, what did you do! "Yes, I did..."

"He messaged me what you said."

I rubbed my forehead, my palms beginning to sweat as I went over the message in my mind. There can always be light, no matter how dark the situation. Please don't give up. I haven't given up on you. There's always hope. Please remember that. I love you.

I slapped my head. I said I love you! Why did I have to say that? I bet it totally looks wrong when you read it!

Jonathan never sounded so serious—apart from when he said he wanted to remain abstinent at the restaurant the other night. "I wanted to hear you out before I listened to what he said."

Oh please, God, salvage this terrible mistake. Heart thrashing wildly, I braced myself as I began. "Okay, I was on his page, and I read something he wrote that was very dark so I felt bad and wanted to give him hope. So I told him God loves him and that I love him, but I didn't mean it in that way. I just meant as a person. I don't wanna be with him like that. I love you."

Still dead serious, Jonathan asked, "Are you sure?"

"I'm positive. I'll never talk to him again if that'll prove to you that I love and want only you." Tears ran down my cheeks. Please, God, don't let this break us. I had hope that Jonathan might be the one You wanted me to marry someday.

"That's what I thought when I read it, but he was trying to say otherwise. And he said a lot of messed up things about you. It really makes me wanna punch him in the face."

My own blood boiled. "What did he say?"

"I don't even wanna tell you."

Anger and regret swelled inside me. This is what I get for trying to help Dace? Him trying to ruin things between Jonathan and I?

"Hold on." I pounded the number pad on my phone as I texted my screwed up ex.

How could you try and break Jonathan and I up? I was just trying to help you. I have never written August a message about you. And by the way, I don't want you as a boyfriend. Sorry if you misinterpreted my message. I hope you feel better, Dace. Take care.

I also swiftly deleted the picture of us and then put the phone to my ear. "Okay, hello?"

"Yeah."

"I'm so sorry," I said as I reentered my room. "I shouldn't have tried to help him. I just need to pray for him. I texted him saying I don't want him as a boyfriend, that I'm sorry if he misinterpreted the message and deleted our picture."

Jonathan's tone softened. "Thank you."

"No problem. I love you, Jonathan."

"I love you too, Natasha."

I lay down, my heartbeat finally starting to slow. Gosh, I feel like Satan's attacking our relationship. He must not want us together. But I love how God can use what was intended for evil for 'the good of those who love Him.' I don't know if Jonathan is the one, but apparently, God doesn't want what we have to end just yet.

10. THE COINCIDENCE AND THE COMPROMISE

"I honestly can't believe you came with me to wait for Twilight to release on DVD." I hugged Jonathan as we stood in the growing Walmart line, anticipating the moment the cashier brings out the epic love movie. But most of all, thankful that he forgave me for the stupidity I pulled two days ago, messaging He Who Shall Not Be Named.

"I don't mind." Jonathan tightened his hold around me. "It's an excuse to hang out with you for two hours."

I smiled as I let him go. "It's really not as packed as I assumed it would be."

"The line's growing gradually."

I looked behind us. About twenty people waited for the special seventeen-dollar release the majority women—with a few men sprinkled in. Several of the ladies stood alone, or with another woman.

My heart ached as I watched them. Here they are, standing in line to get the most romantic movie of the year, probably wishing they had an Edward and hoping to someday have one—if they even believe Edwards exist—and here I am with Jonathan, a dream prince of my own, who —in my opinion—really is better than Edward. I mean, if they seriously thought about it, would they really want a guy like the sparkly vampire? A guy so obsessed with them to the point where if they were to die, he'd have nothing else to live for so he'd kill himself?

In the real world, guys that make a girl their universe end up becoming jealous, possessive, abusive, or all three. And what pains me the most is probably more than half—if not all—of these beautiful women don't even know their worth. That they're an absolute treasure and can have exactly what they need: unconditional love. The kind of love that doesn't leave bruises and scars, and they can obtain it, but by one Man alone. They're princesses. I just pray someday they find out that in order to get their prince, they need to become daughters of the King and give Him their heart first.

I focused on the blonde standing beside us as Jonathan wrapped his arms around my waist. A silver band with engraving on the outside shined on her index finger. Oh my gosh.

I released Jonathan. "Excuse me, is that a purity ring?"

The blonde looked down at her hand. "Yes it is."

"Do you mind if I see it?"

"Sure." She took it off and handed it to me.

"True. Love. Waits." I read the words aloud before handing the ring to Jonathan. "This is exactly what I was telling you about!"

He smiled as he examined it. "This is really cool. Now I really want us to get them."

"I was just trying to show him a purity ring at the bookstore in my church two days ago," I told the woman as he gave it back to her, "but it was closed."

"That's strange," she said.

"It is. What are the chances that the person right behind us in line for the Twilight DVD two days later would be wearing one?"

"They seem slim." She smiled as Jonathan held me.

He whispered. "I think God wanted to remind us to get them."

I smiled as his lips met my forehead. "I agree."

✳✳✳

February was the worst and the best month of my life, the way God saved the day, showering His healing love over me. Then March had quickly become the second best month of my life, meeting the boy of my dreams and becoming his girlfriend, falling in love nearly as fast as Jacob fell for Rachel. And now here I am, in April, experiencing the best first six weeks of a relationship I've ever had with the best boyfriend I've ever had.

The sun beamed from above, its bright rays reflecting off the sea behind Letub's restaurant, paving what looked like a fluorescent sidewalk leading to the end of the horizon. The wind carried a soft breeze that brushed Jonathan's black hair back as we sat at a table under a palm tree. He smiled at me as his eyes glimmered in the afternoon light. Now is the perfect time to show him the book.

"Close your eyes," I said as I removed the leather notebook from my purse.

"More surprises?" Jonathan crooned.

"It's your birthday, of course there's going to be more." I laid it on the table in front of him. "Okay, open them."

His gaze landed on the book. As he opened it and saw the picture I pasted on the inside cover of us, a smile lit up his face. He turned the page. "A poem?"

"There's twenty in there, since you're twenty now."

"'My heart's song.'" Jonathan's silky voice made the poem I wrote sound all the more swooney. "'There's a song in my heart that beats to the rhythm of matrimony, accompanied by a picture in my mind, an aisle adorned with rose petals, a white dress, and a dream prince of a groom. My heart sings perfect notes to such a wonderful truth, awakening my soul to the longing of that day. The day when our two hearts become one and nothing less of my all is gifted to you. For only in you do I see all the wishes I've ever wished in a man come true, all the dreams I've ever dreamt of love made real. And now that my soul has found you, I can only be complete on the day I say, 'I do.'" His stare found mine and like a magnetic pull, he leaned in, drawing me to his lips.

My eyes closed as Jonathan's tender kiss, so genuinely loving, took me to another place. A distant land beyond the glistening shore where only the two of us—he suddenly drew back. Something ablaze in his eyes sent a chill through me. I'd seen that look before…did I cross a line…?

The brightness from the sun faded, reeling in the twilight. Oh no. I grabbed my phone. It's 6:30! The park closes at seven!

I pulled out my wallet and slapped cash onto the table before rising to my feet. "Okay, we have to go."

"Where?"

I grinned. "It's a surprise."

✳✳✳

"Keep them closed," I said to Jonathan as the elevator in which we stood stopped on the fifth floor. The doors opened, revealing the amazing view of the mangrove with the nature trail in the midst of four lakes. The sun began to set, a blend of purple, pink, gold, and blue in the sky. We got here at the perfect time. Thank You, God. "Okay, you can open them."

"Wow." Jonathan took my hand and walked toward the railing. His eyes glowed with admiration as he peered at me. "You're perfect. You're truly a princess, my Aurora."

My heart sang as he gazed out at the mangrove.

"This place is beautiful. I wish I found it first so I could've introduced it to you." Jonathan released my hand as he faced me.

I pulled back, my hands beginning to shake. "There's something else." My throat dried as I gestured for him to sit down. Oh man, this isn't going to be good. Is there a water fountain nearby? Or maybe I can just do this another time.

Jonathan observed me stew as he sat, patiently waiting.

"Can you close your eyes please?" I trembled as he kindly obliged. Please, Jesus, help me. I really wanna do this for him, but I'm so nervous that I'm going to sound bad.

Just do it.

I wavered, fear locking me in place.

You can.

I took in a deep breath and then began to sing. "At last my love has come along. My lonely days are over, and life is like a song. At last, the skies above are blue. My heart was wrapped up in clover, the night I looked at you."

Jonathan's eyes opened, a smile curling the ends of his lips.

My heart floated as I squeezed my eyes shut and continued my weak rendition of

Etta James' masterpiece. "I found a dream that I could speak to. A dream that I can call my own." I fought through all the way until the grand belted finish and then finally, slowly opened my eyes as Jonathan walked toward me.

He cupped my cheeks. "You really do blow every girl I've ever met out of the water." He smiled and then kissed me as the night cloaked us.

***

Tears welled in my eyes. They distorted Jonathan's distraught face as we sat in his car in shameful silence outside of my house. How could I have been so selfish? How could I have hurt him, and even more importantly, how could I have allowed myself to hurt God?

My cheeks turned sticky as the tears dried on them. "I'm so sorry, Jonathan."

"It's not your fault, I should have stopped it."

"It is my fault, I enticed you."

He bowed his head.

Not being able to bear the guilt on his face, I did the same as I replayed it all in my mind. After leaving the observation tower, we sat in this very car and kissed—a little too much. Next thing I knew, I was revealing what lay under my shirt, and the kissing grew to second base. I winced the image away. "It's both of our faults."

Jonathan spoke with that resolute tone, but now a brokenness marred it. "We just have to be stronger."

"I know. I can't believe how weak I am. No wonder Paul says, 'with every temptation God will provide a way of escape.' It's so hard to resist. It's like the only way to fight it is to run away." I dared to look at him. The sullenness of disgrace still dimmed his usually glimmering eyes. The ugliness of our own sin has sullied the innocence of our being in love. If I didn't know how forgiving and understanding God is, I don't know how I'd be able to deal with myself right now.

Jonathan gazed up at me. "Maybe we should practice not touching at all for a week or so."

"I think that's a good idea." I wiped my cheeks and opened the car door. "Goodnight, Jonathan."

"Goodnight, Natasha."

I stepped outside and strode to my porch. I need to practice some self-control. For some reason, I'm weak when temptation beckons me with its alluring, exfoliated and manicured hand. Well, not anymore. After this week of abstaining from kissing, I should be stronger. I won't hurt Jonathan or God again. I refuse to.

***

A bright smile lit up Jonathan's face—a forgiven smile—as we pulled up to the ginormous Dolphin Mall. I smiled with him. I think we both can say we've been smiling a lot since the aftermath of our mistake a few nights ago. If I can pick one thing I love most about my Father in heaven, it would be His immeasurable capacity to forgive.

Jonathan parked the car and turned to me, that beautiful smile still on his mouth. "Close your eyes."

"Ooh, I love surprises!" I said as I heeded.

Taking my hand, he slid a ring onto my index finger. "Okay."

I opened my eyes and instantly squealed. Two silver wedding bands interlocked with one thicker than the other. The engraving on the thicker band's surface read, *I'll wait for you.* Jonathan's name, along with, *TLW* engraved the thinner band.

I caressed it like Gollum and the precious. "Oh my gosh, Jonathan, this is so nice!"

His smiled widened, a red box in his lap.

"May I?" I asked.

"Of course." He handed it to me.

Inside lay a ring identical to mine, except that it had my name engraved on the thinner band. I beamed as I fit it onto his index finger.

"It fits better here." Jonathan took it off and placed it on his ring finger. He peered at me, his eyes agleam. "I love you."

"I love you too, Jonathan." I leaned in.

"Wait."

"Oh yeah." I pouted as I pulled away.

Jonathan wore his resolute voice. "We have to be strong."

I dropped back into my seat as he stepped outside. And yet, I'm apparently still very, very weak because this just sucks for my flesh on so many levels.

Jonathan walked around and opened the passenger for me. "Let's get going, the movie's gonna start soon."

I followed beside him as the night rolled in. Man, this is harder than I thought. But please, God, help me to be strong. I wanna honor You. Just teach me how.

11. SHATTERED DREAMS

I can't wait for this show to be over.

I pulled into the parking lot at Honey's in Dad's Intrepid, the dusk quickly fading to night above me. My jittery hands thrummed against the wheel. Tomorrow's the big day. But it's going to be okay, Natasha. You've rehearsed Seussical with the kids for almost nine months now. If for some random reason any of them were to get sick, you could play their part since you know every line in the show. You're gonna love it, their parents are gonna love it, Jonathan's gonna love it...

"So, we're discussing courtship," a man seemingly well along in age spoke through the radio, his voice kind and wise, like a sage. "I know in your book you talk about a 'spiritual father.' What is a spiritual father?"

"A spiritual father is a pastor," a middle-aged, but still pretty sagey sounding man replied, "or simply a God-fearing man or married couple that looks over your relationship from the outside perspective and helps you out with things you may not see from the inside."

I parked and turned up the interesting broadcast.

"When you're in a relationship, emotions are involved, and sometimes this can cause blindness to certain things, whereas, someone on the outside, who isn't emotionally involved in the relationship, can point out those things. And it's preferable not to have the spiritual father be your actual father because for instance, with my daughter, no man's good enough." He chuckled with the host. "Or any family member because family can be biased, they can be blind to even your faults because they're used to how you 'just are' and there is also the fear of possibly hurting you. They want to avoid family strife whereas someone who isn't related to you doesn't have those fears and biases."

"So then a pastor, like you said, would probably be the most ideal spiritual father?"

"Yes sir, I believe so."

I shut off the car as Honey propped open the front door and then waved at me, her bleach blonde hair and pretty blue-eyed face like Barbie's. Hmm. Spiritual father. I should talk to Jonathan about that…

I hurried inside the studio. The end of the year meeting was officially in session, and hopefully, after tomorrow night's show, I'd still have a job.

"Hello, hello, my beautiful director!" Honey gave me a squeeze and a Barbie-doll smile as she unclipped an hour's sheet from a clipboard she carried. "Are you excited for your big solo debut tomorrow?"

I clasped the paper tightly. "I definitely am, among other things…"

Her highly animated face seemed to implode around her nose. "Oh, sweetheart, it's going to be great!" She waved the clipboard toward the small dance store crammed in between the lobby and the office. "Come, come, I've gotta start this meeting."

I joined all the teachers gathered in a circle on the floor with their hour's sheet in hand—all but one.

"Okay, guys." Honey sat Indian-style on the floor in the middle of the group. "Write in the squares the hours and days you wanna work for next fall."

I jotted in the same hours I worked earlier this year: Monday 5:30pm, Thursday 4:30pm, and Saturday 10am. Hopefully Dace's Saturday class changes. Seeing him around now that he pretty much hates me isn't very pleasant.

"Hey, everyone, sorry I'm late." A lanky man with black-framed glasses that screamed New York theatre director shuffled into the room.

"Oh please." Honey waved off his apology. "Everyone, this is Paul, the new acro teacher."

New Acro teacher?

"New acro teacher?" Fred, the always colorfully-clothed hip-hop instructor took the words out of my mind. "Does that mean Dace left?"

"Yes he…" She shook her head and cringed like she'd just seen a spider get crushed. "Anyways, we're just filling in our desired hours for next…"

I tried to focus as she repeated the information Paul missed. Wow…this means I won't have to see Dace twice a week. God must have known seeing him often now that he disdains me isn't very good for me emotionally, and that it also isn't very good for Jonathan and I's relationship. I mean, I love my boyfriend, but the heart is deceitful —who can really know it? I've let my emotions get the best of me many times before and the outcome was never a pretty one. But I'm so flipping done with that now.

I know better than to let my emotions lead my decisions.

I set my request sheet for my hopefully same hours at the same job down and listened to Honey the Barbie share her dreams for the upcoming year.

***

My skin crawled as I sat in Natalia's room before the computer. Did this inappropriate Facebook conversation really happen earlier?

Hey there. The striking redhead with villainous, icy blue eyes, Ember Easley, posted on Jonathan's wall.

For reasons I'm still trying to understand, he wrote back. *What's up?*

Nothing really. I was looking at your pictures— the ones from you and your cousin on Halloween— and they're hilarious. Do you want to pursue acting after college?

I'm more into writing and directing. I like acting, but I just went into the theatre program because I think knowing how to act helps when directing. What about you?

Yeah, I agree. I definitely want to pursue acting after BCC.

So this redhead is in the theatre program with him? Wonderful. I forced myself to keep reading her post.

I actually want to try and transfer to New World after my sophomore year. But you seem really cool, like someone I'd have deep conversations with about life. I'll message you my number. Feel free to call me whenever.

Okay cool.

"What! Okay cool?" I stalked away from the computer. All right, don't let your emotions get the best of you, 'Anger never produces the righteousness of God.' But this Ember fifi is totally trying to get with my boyfriend! I grabbed my phone off of Natalia's unmade bed and called Kelly.

"Hello?"

"Girl, listen to this." I plopped into the computer chair and reread the disturbing and completely unnecessary conversation to her.

"Okay yeah," she said. "Her intentions definitely don't seem innocent. I've dealt with that with Arieus, but maybe her motives aren't to get him."

"Kelly. You don't understand, this fifi has been blowing up his page. She's even commented his photos!"

She laughed. "Fifi?"

"Fifi, as in female." I turned away from the screen. "I don't trust this fiery redhead."

"Well, tell Jonathan how you feel, but don't tell him when you're upset. Just calm down, pray about it, and then talk to him."

I heaved in a sigh. Pray about it. That sounds like a good idea—one I have yet to consider. "Okay. Thanks, girl."

"No problem. I'll be praying for you."

"Thank you. I love you, Kels."

"I love you, too. Now go talk to our Heavenly Father."

"All right."

"Bye, sister."

I placed the phone down and did what I should've done immediately after I saw the conversation. "Please, Jesus, if this girl doesn't have good intentions, protect Jonathan from her. I pray that she comes to know You, and finds her own man. And help me to be calm when I talk to him about it. Please. Thank you. I love you. Amen." I inhaled slowly as I called Jonathan.

"Hi, earth angel."

My grip on the phone tightened. "Hi, dream prince."

"What are you up to?"

Anger and annoyance quickly resurfaced in my heart. "I was just on your Facebook, and I saw the conversation on your wall between you and Ember. I think she likes you."

"I don't think she likes me. She's new to the theatre program, she's probably just trying to make friends. I'm not the only one she comments I'm sure."

"Does she give other guys in the program her number so they can have, 'deep conversations about life'?"

"I don't know, ask her."

The fiery emotions within me burned stronger. "Are you really that naïve? You're gorgeous and she's single."

"You went to her page? Babe, really, I think you're blowing things out of proportion."

"I know a snake when I read one."

"Maybe she's a Russian spy and I'm her mission, and this is the last thing you say to me before she kills me."

"How would you like it if I had a friendly public conversation with a guy who gave me his number so we can have 'deep conversations about life' together?"

"So I can't have a deep conversation with anyone, but you?"

"Sure you can, with fellow males."

"I don't wanna live my life that way."

"Okay, Jonathan. Fine. She doesn't like you, you're right. Have a nice convo with your beautiful redhead platonic female friend. I have to go now."

"Okay, whatever, bye."

I slammed my thumb against the end call button. Tears piled up as I strode out of Natalia's room and into my own. I thought I could trust Jonathan. Maybe I was wrong.

***

"So this is that guy from my acting class I told you about." Natalia sat beside me at the kitchen island, her iPhone screen displaying a tall, shirtless metrosexual with the ocean glittering behind him. "His name is Mauricio. I'm seeing him now. He's fine, right?" Marijuana soured her breath.

A rock weighed my heart down. From age twelve to nineteen, that "gateway drug" had been her fave. Pills to alcohol and everything in between, Nati had done it all and barely dragged herself through high school. But the one thing my family liked about her husband was his ultimatum: get clean or he'd get lost. And she did. She even miraculously finished night school and graduated and went to college, pursuing her dreams of acting.

But then the bubble popped. Imperfect love can only tame a wild and lost heart for so long. When their conditional love failed, so did her promise and resolve to abstain from previous pleasures.

Guy after guy. Drunken and high night after drunken and high night, Nati hadn't gotten any better—but worse. I grew up watching my big sister ruin her teen years, and here I am five years later, witnessing her destroy her early adulthood.

"Nati…" my voice ached with the pain and love Jesus had for her. "You're not going to find what you're looking for in a guy."

"Says the good girl who's all in love with Jonathan now." She set her phone on the counter. "The guy I introduced you to."

"Yes, but I don't need Jonathan nor was I looking for him. I was content with Jesus."

"I'm never going to be like you!" She shoved out of the stool and roared in my face like a lioness whose cubs were threatened. "I'm still going to cuss, I'm still going to smoke and drink. I'm going to find God my own way!" She snatched her cell and stamped to her bedroom, slamming the door so hard I nearly felt it in my skin.

Tears piled in my eyes as I bounded to my own room. I fell to my knees and whispered through tears, "Oh, Father, I'm losing hope for her. I just can't picture Natalia ever giving her life to You. She's so hard and angry...But nonetheless I pray. I pray one day she will be a Bible-believing, purity-ring wearing, non-cussing, sold-out-for-Jesus, 'Christian like me.' Somehow, work a miracle in Nati's life, please, in Jesus' name..."

Head in my hands, I continued to pray as thunder rumbled in the distance.

✳✳✳

Why in the world would he do that if he loves me so much? I can't imagine what would possess him to commit such a stunt, but it sure as heaven ain't my Heavenly Father! I sat up in my bed and texted Jonathan back. I don't think Jesus would approve of his decision whatsoever.

Are you serious, Jonathan? Why on earth would you go to the movies with Ember and some friends of hers that you don't even know? We just had a conversation of how I feel about her last week.

I can't believe this is happening. Does he like her or something? Is he bored of me already and wants someone new? He did admit once before Ember showed up in his acting class that he found redheads attractive. I thought he was my dream prince, but he's acting like a foolish jester! My phone chimed.

Yeah, but I really don't think she wants to be more than friends. And it's not like we're going alone.

"Oh, so just because he's not going alone with her that makes it okay?" I pounded my keypad.

Fine. I can't make you do anything. Ttyl.

I put my cell on silent and shoved it under my pillow, tears beginning to coat my cheeks. "God, please help me be strong. Help me be able to sleep tonight. Please speak to me. I need You." I grabbed my Bible off the head-rest and opened it to any page.

It is better to take refuge in the Lord than to trust in princes.—Psalm 118:9

I chuckled despite my messed up situation. Goodness, my Father never fails me with His Word. I sighed, good and long, the tremulous wrath easing out of my limbs. "You're right, God. I'm sorry. Jonathan is a prince, but he's not a perfect King like You. He's gonna let me down. Thank You so much for answering me, for seeing me, as You always do." The quiet peace of God's presence rested on my shoulders and the tears stopped rolling. I closed my eyes and allowed perfect Love to help me briefly forget my earthly, imperfect one.

***

A vibrating prodded me out of my nap. I felt for my phone in the dark. *My Dream Boy.*

A softer tremor—thanks to Christ alone—but still spicy enough, charged through me. "How was your group date?"

"I'm sorry, Natasha." Jonathan's sappy voice did sound genuine.

I'm gonna forgive him for going to the movies with the red-headed snake—after I discover what possessed him to go. "Do indulge me, why did you choose to accept her invite?"

"I don't know I guess…I just thought there might've been something between me and her."

A much stronger tremor raged through my body. Lord, help me. I jolted upright. "Pardon me?"

"There was something there…" Shame responded…"But not the something I wanted." Resolute replied.

Though my hand threatened to break my phone in a thoroughly dramatic way that involved my wall, I kept it to my ear and inhaled, my breath shaky. I shut out the bright reds in my room, blazing like my blood. *Heavenly, Father, I can't even talk right now. I need your help because I'm about ready to let my Cuban lead and ju—*

"When I was with her tonight…I just… didn't feel the way I feel when I'm with you."

Still at an extreme loss for words, I exhaled into the phone, like Smaug before he went off on Bilbo. "Uh huh."

"I felt…guilty tonight. Like I committed a crime. Right when I got home and went to my room, I fell to my knees and asked God to forgive me. I know I did wrong by Him— and by you." Jonathan's tone echoed the brokenness it had when we messed up in his car a few weeks ago—a mess up I partook in and even helped provoke. "I don't know what came over me…but I'm never doing that again."

Another exhale leaked from my nostrils, but this time, my anger melted. "I forgive you, Jonathan."

"Really?"

"I mean, nothing else happened, right?"

"No, nothing happened."

"Okay, so yes, I forgive you." Though because of Jesus, even if something did go down, I'd still have to pardon him—but sure as heaven wouldn't have to stay with him.

"That feels good to hear," Jonathan said, a little lighter. "Thank you."

I sighed again, my eyes upward toward where my Perfect Prince sat on a throne of unconditional love and endless mercy. Though it totally sucks being hurt by the guy I love and trust so much, I know I'm not perfect either. I've messed up already in this relationship and hurt both him and God. And seeing as neither of us have received our perfect, immortal bodies, I expect we'll be messing up some more.

O, God, we need You and Your grace to carry us through to the other side…

12. THE BOOK

I love the feeling of Jonathan's hand twined in mine. I squeezed tighter, eyes on my parents' new flat screen TV. Kirk Cameron's fire-fighter friend in *Fireproof* encouraged Kirk's character in what I hope to someday share with Jonathan…

"Man, God made marriage to be for life…And you can't just follow your heart man, because your heart can be deceived. But you gotta lead your heart."

I cocked my head. Huh, lead your heart? I never heard that one before. If only I did way back in Kindergarten. Following your heart is super deceiving—hence my fifty-two failed relationships prior to my dream prince. Yes, I totally count the year-long relationship with Bobby Well when I was six because I cried over it. That little emotionally-charged fling was so legit. It sparked a decade long feud with that twice-my-size bully I fought in sixth grade. And that's what happens when you follow your heart—it leads your feisty, Cuban little fists flying over a boy who ate his boogers.

I studied Jonathan, all kinds of bubbly, fluffy feelings swarming in my stomach. He's not perfect—not that anyone is, except Jesus —but no guy has ever treated me like he does. And although he made me cry over the whole Ember debacle, I cried a lot more in my past relationships. Heck, ninety percent of those catastrophes were spent in tears. But with Jonathan, it's like the majority of our relationship is making one another happy...

"I can't wait to marry you someday." The words flowed from my lips—perhaps a little too easily.

Jonathan's hypnotizing greens settled onto mine. "I can't wait to marry you someday six years from now."

I clenched my jaw, the warm and fluffy feelings dropping dead in my gut. Five or six years...? "Like when you're twenty-six and I'm twenty-five?"

"Yeah, I just wanna finish college, get a job, before I jump off that cliff, you know?"

I whacked his bicep and he chuckled softly.

"I'm just kidding. I'll jump off a cliff with you anytime." His chuckling fell off the map. "But I would like to wait around six years. That part's not a joke."

"Um…" I slowly turned the remote over in my hand. "How can we wait that long… to be…one?"

Now those hypnotic greens turned pensive. "When I came up with that plan in the past I guess I didn't think about waiting till marriage…since you're the first girl I've chosen to wait for. Maybe we can just be super strong and try to be as least romantic with each other as possible. Like we're best friends who are secretly in love with each other."

I scowled at him like my grandma would if I opened the fridge without asking. "That's not gonna work."

"I agree. That's why I have a back-up plan."

I crossed my arms. "You clearly do not since I wasn't part of your original plan."

The tiniest crease formulated on his brow. "I do I just…have to figure out what it is."

Lovely. I forced my eyes back on the TV. Yes, we totally have some spiritual growing to do—and I am still struggling with some of his Catholic beliefs that don't align with the Bible he still has yet to read—but I don't think it'll take that long. At least…I hope it won't…

***

I stood by the small bookshelf in Meg's quaint, a-touch-of-hobbit-hole-looking living room as she walked out the last girl who'd attended her Bible study. Summer's afternoon high beams saturated the space, illuminating all the rich, Christian literature.

God did it: He sent me even more help from His sanctuary, as He promised He would when I threw open my Bible on February 22nd and stumbled upon Psalm 20.

Seek and you shall find. After God answered my prayer and sent Kelly, I took that verse to heart and began seeking more Christian friends. Attending that women's Bible study at church and meeting the twenty-one-year-old ballet dancer has helped me so much.

"How'd you like the study?" Meg reentered her living room in all her tall, slender, ballerina glory. Cinnamon curls bouncing, shoulders straight, her steps far more graceful than mine will ever be, she joined me by her bookcase.

"I absolutely loved it, Meg, thanks so much for inviting me."

"It's one-hundred-percent my joy and privelege, truly." Her warm, brown eyes lowered to a middle shelf. She removed a book and handed it to me. "I wanna give you this."

I read the simple-looking, black-and-white cover. *Choosing God's Best: Wisdom for Lifelong Romance* by Dr. Don Raunikar.

"I felt like I needed to give this to you. Give it back whenever. I don't need it at the moment, but I read it, and it's really good. It's about courtship."

Courtship. I heard the term on that radio station. And I totally failed to mention it to Jonathan like I'd planned…With finishing up Seussical and things going so well with us—minus a few things like a possible, hyper-extended engagement and clashing beliefs—it must've slipped my mind.

I held the book to my chest. "Thanks, Meg, I really appreciate it."

"Not a problem. How are you and Jonathan by the way?"

I drummed my fingers against the book. "We're good. God just kind of revealed to me through something that happened that I need to be more of a friend to him."

"Ah." Meg nodded as she pointed her thin finger at *Choosing God's Best*. "This book talks about that. It breaks it down into stages. The first stage you're not very affectionate and touchy, like, at all."

My face warmed and I knew for sure my Snow White complexion threw me under the bus. After our week-long touching fast, we kinda dove right back into the swoon-worthy kissing sessions and hold-on-forever hug fests, and the can't-let-your-hand-go every time we walk happenings. But at least we hadn't fumbled into second base again, although admittedly, it's not been easy.

Megan overlooked my blushing—perhaps genuinely oblivious. "You just build the friendship aspect of the relationship. Then the spiritual—going to church together, reading the Word together, praying together, serving together, and lastly, the physical. But with the physical you build up to holding hands, hugging, and kissing, nothing beyond that. In essence, it's preparing you for marriage."

Face now probably twins with Bob the Tomato, I shook my head. "Wow. I've never done friendship first. I mean, with that one French guy sort of, but that's just because I had no idea one day we'd be boyfriend and girlfriend. I was his friend because that's how

I viewed him at first. But with guys I like, it's always physical and emotional primarily. Only with my last ex and Jonathan was there a spiritual aspect. But Dace's was negative. Jonathan is different—even though he hasn't been coming to church with me lately, he just goes to his Catholic Church…"

Meg walked over to her orange loveseat where my purse still lay, plopped down, and then patted the space beside her. "Come into my office."

I chuckled as I joined her, slipping the book into my purse. "We say grace together sometimes, but I wouldn't consider that really investing time in prayer. And reading the Bible together? He bought a Bible, but he doesn't read it often. I know how important it is, but he says he doesn't need to read it all the time to get closer to God, that volunteering at his church and praying draws him closer to God." I shifted in my seat, my heart suddenly turning heavy. I almost feel like Jonathan has more of a relationship with the Catholic Church than he actually does with Jesus Himself. "Yeah… I really need to talk to him about all this."

"Pray about it."

"Yes, I definitely will."

Megan gave me one of her tight, big-sis squeezes and then bounced in the chair like a kid hyped on candy. "You're going to Romania soon! Are you excited?"

My heart sped up at the mention of my very first mission's trip. "Yes, ma'am."

"You're gone for ten days right?"

"Yeah, I can't wait. The moment the church announced they were going to Romania to bring hope to the orphans over there, I wanted to go."

"That's awesome, I'll be praying for you, girl. God's going to do some great things!"

The surreal reality of my rapidly approaching trip lightened the weight from the whole Jonathan situation. Just to be away for ten days with no cell phone or any other distractions, purposing to bring children the love of Jesus, is going to be life transforming —I know it.

After another squeeze from Meg, and my new book in tote, I started the semi-long drive back to Miami. I really can't wait for Romania. I believe God is going to do some incredible things, and I have a feeling I'm gonna experience Him on this trip like never before.

My heart burned with excitement. I love Jonathan, but I'll have to contemplate my situation with him when I come back home.

13. THE WISE ADVICE

I set down the book I'd been reading about being a godly wife, and shifted my sights out of the old bus's window. Grassy hills and farmlands folded into one another, bathed in sunlight and bordered by dense forests and towering mountains. I can't believe I'm in Oradea, Romania. Without all the buildings and artificial lights it's so much easier to see God's beauty, to sense how big He is, and how He truly does encompass all things with Himself.

Spiritual father.

The small voice in my mind quickened my blood flow, the adrenaline placing me on alert-mode. Another term I'd heard on that radio broadcast—and still haven't spoken to Jonathan about.

I looked to my right where one of the few men in our team sat on the edge of his seat, his blonde hair almost white in the early morning brightness. Mike?

No.

I looked at kind, balding, perhaps in his early fifties, Matt. How about Matt?

No.

I glanced at the front of the bus as it slowed to a stop. Pastor John stood by the door, his dark goatee highlighting his bright smile as he laughed with our Romanian bus driver. Pastor John?

Yes.

Okay, let's test if this is really You, Lord. I got out of my seat and ambled toward Pastor John as the bus door opened. "Hey, Pastor John."

He directed his friendly smile at me, his teeth extra white against his sun-burned face. "What's goin' on?"

I followed him outside to the tiny gas station that looked like something out of a dystopian flick. "Do you know what a spiritual father is?"

"Yes I do."

I slid my hands into my jean pockets. "Have you ever been a spiritual father?"

"A few times."

The adrenaline coursing inside me strengthened. "Well…I have a boyfriend… and I really love him, but we're not considering marriage anytime soon, but I mean, if we ever get to that level, will you be our spiritual father?"

Pastor John grabbed a bag of chips. "Of course. When we get back we can make plans to sit down, and I could meet him and we can discuss courtship and purity."

"Okay. Thanks, Pastor John!" I jumped, nearly knocking over a stand of magazines and garnering sideways looks from the hooded cashier.

"No problem. Just keep praying about it and be patient." Pastor John gave my shoulder a pat. "Let God do it."

I smiled as I skipped back to the bus. I guess that was You.

***

I've never prayed so much in my entire life. I knelt down beside one of the twelve twin-sized beds in the dark cabin, every inch of my body aching from the thirteen mile hike we took through the mountains and caves of Oradea a few hours earlier. I don't go to the gym so apart from being a weakling, my stomach has been a raging lion, perturbed by any and everything I eat. I don't know if it was food poisoning or my body is just shocked at all the non-processed food, but the last three days have been brutal.

"In all things, pray." Maggie, our sweet nurse encouraged me earlier before embarking on our trek. And so we did. Right outside in the path, surrounded by woods, the group of kids and the few missionaries who'd decided to brave the mountains patiently standing ahead. And miraculously, my tortuous indigestion kept itself at bay—for fourteen hours—hill after hill, step after step, even on up into a cold cave. My dread of having to go number two in the woods with nothing but leaves to wipe with hadn't panned out.

Every time my gut threatened to explode, I set my hands upon it and prayed. Every time my legs begged me to turn back, I prayed. The physical covering was amazing, but it was just enough to keep me utterly dependent on God—and a walking stick.

"I just wanna thank You again, God, for sustaining me the whole way," I whispered so I wouldn't awaken the women sleeping near me. "Now I understand what Paul meant when he said, 'pray without ceasing.' I believe if I hadn't prayed as much as I did, I would've collapsed from exhaustion."

I closed my eyes and continued my nightly prayer routine, going through my list of family and friends and other loved ones.

"And, Lord, I pray for Natalia." Suddenly, the words poured out of my mouth, as if someone pressed the fast-forward button on my prayer. Now that I think of it, the last few nights for some weird reason, whenever I got to Nati, my praying did become faster…more urgent…

My blood stirred, accelerating my heartbeat. The words I shared with Ashley on the bus ride here to the cabins came to mind. *"I've been praying to experience God more. I know this trip is one of the ways I'm going to, and I've also been praying the last four months for the gift of tongues."*

I'm getting the gift of tongues!

I held back a squeal as I sat straighter, though continued to whisper. "Yes, Lord. I know what You're doing, and I say yes to Your Spirit, Father."

A cool wind trickled into my fingers, dispersing itself into my palms, moving as though it were…alive. I recoiled, fear choking my heart. The wind quickly retreated.

"No wait! I know this is You, Lord. I rebuke my fear. I do want this gift, please give it to me, God."

The lively wind returned like a gust. It surged through my hands at a swifter pace than before. The sensation filled my feet, rising to my legs, and then up my arms. I giggled at the unreal goodness of God now literally pouring into me. The breezy rush closed in on my chest and engulfed my heart. My tongue unraveled and began moving on its own accord. Overwhelming joy and peace saturated every inch of my being. Tears streamed from my eyes as I attempted to contain my joy so my sleeping sisters wouldn't be bothered.

My tongue continued to make foreign noises and a whispering of perhaps a language I'd never heard before. Kelly was right! This tongues thing is real! God, You're amazing. I wish I could feel like this forever!

My tongues continued for maybe an hour, the bliss from God's Spirit filling my body still incredibly encompassing, unlike any high I've ever experienced in my life— and I'd had a number senior year and after graduation. The pain from my hike no longer fazed me. I just wanted to sit there at the foot of my small bed and soak in the reality of God's presence for as long as possible.

But finally, the high began to fade, and my tongue slowed to a normal pace. A small whisper reached my ear. I squinted in the darkness to my left. Ashley sat up in bed, her head bowed in prayer! Heart still overloaded with joy, I tiptoed her way. "Ashley!"

"Natasha?"

"Yes, I'm so sorry to interrupt, but I just had to share with someone, and it's so crazy that you're the only one on this trip that I shared this desire with, and you're the only one awake right now, but I just got tongues!"

"That's amazing, Natasha, I was praying you'd get it!"

In the dark, I could just barely make out her kind brown eyes and tender smile.

"Thank you so much, Ashley, really." I gave her a hug and then crawled back to my bed. I knew this trip was going to be life changing. After all that I've experienced here —especially the change in the kids, once so hard and hopeless and now eyes shining and faces always smiling; the great love of my new friends, and now this—the gift of tongues—I don't ever wanna leave.

The day's events finally laid hold of me, and I closed my eyes on the best night I've ever had.

✳✳✳

The sun sank behind a mountain as the bus drove away from the camp. Tears welled as I remembered the hugging and weeping shared amongst the team and the children as they left us yesterday to go back to the Child Placement Center. Even the older, rougher kids wept and clung to us, not wanting to let go…

I rubbed my eyes and forced the memory out of my mind. They all will be in my prayers, and hopefully, some day we'd all meet again, in heaven…

As the mountains grew further and further away, a new thought rose: I'm going to see Jonathan tomorrow. It'd been ten whole days without a single text or call. How was he?

I grabbed my bag beside me and took out a pen and my little purple journal.

August 1st, 2009

Now that the kids are gone, I can think about Jonathan. I miss his hugs and his voice…But over this trip I've learned a lot. And although I've said it before, I really want to be less physical with him. I don't want to love him because of how he makes me feel when we touch. I want to love him for how God's made him. I want to love him for his heart. I want to hang out with him and his friends. Not just him and I. I'm going to try really hard to avoid that. I'm already in deep emotionally, so I want to hang out around honest people that will tell me what they see from an outsider's perspective. When you're in deep emotionally, you're sometimes blind to things. It's just safe and smart to hang out with others who can tell us about what we might not see: good or bad. And I really pray someday we can have Pastor John as our spiritual father. I hope one day I can marry this boy, but I want to do it the right way.

I closed my journal and focused on the road ahead.

14. SEVERED

"You look beautiful, Mamashmoo," Mom said from the bottom of the staircase as I posed for her from the landing. Even though I felt pretty in my royal purple top that made me feel like a modern day princess, a dull ache crept into my heart. It's weird...I've only been home for three hours, yet I long to be back in Romania, with the kids, with my brothers and sisters in Christ, surrounded by the presence of God, minds focused on Him, and Him alone...

A few knocks jangled our old door.

My knees locked as Mom took her sweet time toward the entry. I haven't laid eyes on Jonathan for ten days. It's so amazing how the image of someone you love can fade from your memory after only a week without seeing them. I clutched the rail as Mom opened the door.

"Come on in." She stepped back.

"Hi, Mrs. Sanchez." Jonathan's deep voice still sounded as melodic as I remembered it. He stepped into the living room, as handsome as ever in a green button down that brought out his gorgeous eyes—now on me.

Suddenly able to move, I trotted down the stairs and threw my arms around him.

"And I'm in front of Cinderella again," he spoke in my ear.

I drew back, taking in the details of his face that I had forgotten while away; the light, almost coral green shade of his irises; the honey, reef-like shape bordering his pupils; the soft pink of his smooth lips. He smiled at me and then pressed his mouth against mine. I reluctantly kissed him. Huh. This doesn't feel as good as it used to.

I quickly released and hugged Mom. "See you later."

"Okay, love you, be safe." She followed us out into the night. "And wear your seatbelts!"

"Thanks for the reminder." I waved as we ambled toward Jonathan's silver Honda. I could feel his eyes on me…

Only a few stars occupied the sky. The tiny lights seemed out of place in their distance from the moon, as if someone set them there against their will.

Jonathan opened the door for me as usual, and then held my hand while we drove away from my house. "How was your trip?"

I sighed as I watched the stars, so dim in comparison to the millions of lights over the dark forest and mountains in Oradea. "It was amazing, really humbling, too. It was so cool to meet people who have a totally different culture than you with not much in common except a love for Jesus. Just how uniting that was and how we all had the same goal. Every day something beautiful happened." The memories of the children and the glorious mountains and star-filled nights that so clearly displayed God's glory gnawed at my heart, bringing back the dull ache.

"Cool," Jonathan replied, his hand warm in mine as it caressed the purity ring I had yet to take off since the time Jonathan put it on me. "That sounds good."

It was so much more than good… "How was your trip to Tallahassee?"

"It was good. I met Andrew up there. We stayed at my brother's house. Every day was an adventure." He chuckled, his eyes ahead. "We're calling the trip, 'Talla-nasty Knights.'"

I jerked my head in his direction. "Pardon me?"

Jonathan chuckled again. "Like the movie Talladega Nights."

"Um yeah, but why talla 'nasty?'"

"I don't know, it's just a nickname people have for Tallahassee. Probably doesn't mean anything good now that I think about it."

"Yeah…probably not."

"My brother graduates soon so we're going up there again. Maybe you can come."

"Yeah, maybe." I stared out the window as Jonathan merged onto the highway. I loosened my hold on his hand, though he didn't let go in the slightest. Why do I suddenly feel so distant from him? Something's…off.

I didn't say a word the rest of the ride to our usual Chinese restaurant as I tried to busy my mind with the passing sceneries, too afraid to think of why I was suddenly feeling strange around my boyfriend despite the fact that I haven't seen him in eleven days.

We arrived at the restaurant after twenty agonizing minutes of silence.

Jonathan clasped my hand again as we walked inside and approached the cashier. As he ordered our food, queasiness disquieted my gut. I let go of his hand again and took a seat at a nearby table while he waited for our meals. Okay, this feeling isn't getting any better. I admit, I hardly thought of Jonathan while I was away, but that was because I barely had any down time and when I did, I took a nap or read my Bible or prayed. But when I was on my way home, I was super excited to see him, yet now I feel like something's wrong...with us.

Jonathan set our plates down and sat across from me. "I played basketball a lot while I was in Tallahassee. I really wanna start playing more again."

I picked up my fork and played with my chicken. Can't we talk about something meaningful...something spiritual?

Break up with him.

I dropped my utensil, heart hammering. "I'm going to the ladies' room real quick." I slipped out of my chair and scurried through a small hallway, and into the bathroom. I stared at myself in the mirror. The bright bulbs exposed tears gathering in my eyes. "Do you really want me to break up with him, God?"

Yes.

The dull ache in my chest from before worsened, as if it were a hole being dug into by an invisible hand. "Please help me do what You want me to. Give me the strength. Your will be done, in Jesus' name. Amen." I wiped my eyes, and after taking a deep breath, walked back to the table. Jonathan smiled at me as I sat down.

You can do this, Natasha. I forced myself to eat as he continued talking about his trip to Tallahassee. He asked me more about Romania, and as I shared my tongues experience that night after the hike, I realized something. Although Jonathan is really sweet and beautiful, and believes in the same God I do, we're not strong spiritually. I've allowed this relationship to go in the same pattern I did with my exes: all romance and affection, with no real substance. It's not as bad because Jonathan's different, but it's still not what God wants it to be…

"You ready to go?" Jonathan's voice sounded afar off and weary…as if he finally picked up that something was wrong…

"Yeah, I am." I kept my head down as we walked back to his car. Although the air felt the same as before, it suddenly gave me chills.

Jonathan wrapped his arm on my shoulder as he escorted me to the passenger side. Lowering his grasp to my waist, he gently pressed me against the door, his body close to mine as he kissed my neck. The sensation that once set my skin on fire, now made it crawl.

With little force, I pushed him away. "I can't do this."

Jonathan dropped his hands. "What do you mean?"

Water flooded my eyes as I sat down on the curb, the cold in the air intensifying. I hesitated as Jonathan sat beside me, my heart turning heavier with every passing second. "We rushed into the physical and built up the emotional first."

He looked at the pavement, his face pale. "Let's go."

"But—"

"I don't want to talk about this here." Jonathan stood and got into the car.

Weakness kept me on the curb as the reality of my situation pounced on my mind —and heart. I can't believe this is happening.

I'm breaking up with Jonathan.

With what strength I could muster, I rose to my feet and entered the passenger. I glanced at him. His eyes glistened with pain as he started the car. My gaze shifted before I could begin weeping. I really thought he was the one for me, but why do I feel the need to do this? To end things with the guy I love? The guy I hoped to marry someday…

It seemed like only minutes and we parked in front of my house. Similar to the stars and moon, I felt distant from Jonathan as he peered at me, eyes still moist with tears yet to have fallen. My weakness, wrought with pain, made looking at him so hard to bear.

"I just can't do this." I grabbed my purse and darted into the house as sorrow swallowed my heart. I cantered up the stairs and collapsed onto my bed. "How did I let myself do this again?" I sobbed into my pillow. "Please God, hold my heart together. Hold his heart together. Show me what You want me to do now. Please."

***

I rolled over on my side, my body sore as I looked at the alarm clock beside my purse: 4:46pm. Thankfully, Mom and Dad are at work still and Natalia's out, because I've been locked up in my room since last night. I haven't prayed this much since my thirteen mile hike in Romania. If I didn't know the immeasurable depth of God's loves for me, I would definitely think He'd be annoyed of all my talking by now.

I sat upright and removed my purse from the headrest and dug through it, feeling around for cold metal. Where the heck is my camera? Tension gripped my heart as I put my purse down. Oh no. I must've left it in Jonathan's car. Dang it. I haven't spoken to him since the breakup.

My hands trembled as I texted him. *I left my camera in your car.*

"'Hi, Jonathan. I know I just broke your heart yesterday, but can you drop my camera off for me?' Wow, Natasha, so smart of you."

My phone vibrated. I won't be surprised if he says, 'I threw it out the window on the way home.'

I'll drop it off for you.

I reread the text. He'll drop it off for me? Why? After what I did to him? I don't even want to see me. And I'm not sure I wanna face him just yet…

Thank you. When can you come?

Now.

I hopped off my bed and dashed into the bathroom to brush my teeth. My puffy eyes and red nose gave away the fact that I'd been crying a lot. Whatever, at least he'll know this decision hurt me, too. Maybe it'll make him feel better.

I bustled back to my bedside and bowed on my knees again. "God, I know I've been asking You all day, but please, show me what You want me to do. I really love Jonathan, but I want to do Your will. Not mine. In Jesus' name, amen."

I threw on a shirt and jeans and pulled my hair back. Your will be done. I can't say that enough. Apparently, I never knew what I was doing in relationships, and I still don't so please help.

My phone vibrated on my bed. I snatched it and quickly opened the text.

I'm outside.

"Goodness. Was he already on his way over here when I texted him?" I trudged downstairs and took a deep breath before opening the front door.

The lavender, twilight sky made me squint as I walked outside. Man, I've been cooped up in the dark for too long. I focused on the silver Honda parked in the grass by the sidewalk.

Jonathan stepped out of the car and approached me as I drew near.

I avoided his eyes. "Hi."

"So you're breaking up with me?" He handed me the camera.

My hands trembled as I made myself look at him. "Yes."

Shoulders squared, he almost looked as if he were ready to brawl—with words of course. "Why?"

The words came forth faster than I could think through them. "Because I fell in love with the romantic side of you and everything except who you are in God. I don't know who you are in Him."

"What do you mean? I have faith. I believe in Him. Sure, maybe I don't read the Bible as much as you do, but I have a relationship with Him."

"Okay, but we barely talk about Him. Our relationship is all about us—dating, hanging out, kissing." I spoke faster. "It's kind of like all my past relationships."

Jonathan gaped at me. "Like all your past relationships? So I'm just like all your exes?"

I stammered. "No, I didn't mean you're like them, you're different. It's just the way we rushed into the physical and romance, and didn't build up our friendship and the spiritual first."

Jonathan glowered now, his tone matching his face. "Whatever, Natasha. If you want me back after this, I don't know if I'll be able to be with you again." He strode back to his car.

I ran after him. "Wait, Jonathan. Please don't leave like this. I don't want to end on this note."

He opened the door.

"Please." Tears filled my eyes as he stared at me, his forehead wrinkled with disappointment, anger, pain...

Jonathan held my gaze and then finally closed the car door. "Okay."

A weight lifted from my heart, though it still dangled heavily within. "Can we go into the backyard?"

"Yeah."

The sky darkened, ushering in the night as we trudged through the metal gate. Jonathan led the way, seating us in the same spot where we had our first kiss...

My shoulders slumped as I looked at him —the man I thought I'd marry someday. His puffy eyelids revealed that he, too, had cried a lot since last night, since I broke his heart without any prior warning.

I shifted my view upward to the ebony sky, the sadness in his gorgeous face unbearable. Gosh I really can't picture myself without him. Please, Jesus, if You want us together give me a sign. Let me see a shooting star or something.

Jonathan gasped. "I just saw a shooting star."

I scanned the skies. But I asked for me to see it. So why did he see it instead? Gosh, I hate being confused! Is this Satan again?

Toying with me? But can he even hear my prayers if I don't speak them aloud?

"You know," Jonathan spoke quietly, "I was preparing something for you, but I think I should do it now, in case I don't get to in the future." He cleared his throat and then faced me. Those green eyes carried so much in them…so much love…for me. Jonathan's lips parted. "I want to make you smile whenever you are sad," he sang the words, "carry you around when your arthritis is bad. Oh, all I wanna do is grow old with you."

I cried as he sang the familiar Adam Sandler song from that sweet movie where he married Drew Barrymoore at the end. He went through every line, its own variation of wedding vows. Caring for the girl when she was too sick to care for herself…putting her before his own desires, providing for her…And though Adam Sandler made himself so endearing in that film, Jonathan, with his gentle, yet strong, heart, his resolution to do the right thing, to honor and love God, and me, made his rendition even better than the A-list actor's.

As I chuckled and cried simultaneously, Jonathan's eyes glistened. "I love you, Natasha."

My chuckling stopped, but the tears didn't. I scooted closer to Jonathan and let my head fall on his shoulder.

Peering up at the stars, I kept my response in my heart.

I love you, too.

15. GET BACK UP AGAIN

I eased off my bed and got onto my knees for what seemed like the fiftieth time. Two days of fasting, praying, and reading the Bible until my eyes hurt, and still no clear answer on what I'm supposed to do regarding Jonathan. I don't know if this is a test of endurance, but if it is, I'll keep waiting on God until He tells me what to do. I refuse to run ahead of Him this time.

"Lord, please give me guidance on what You want me to do. Please. In Jesus' name. Amen." I gathered what little energy I had and flopped back onto my bed. My eyes landed on a book hanging a little off the edge of my headrest bookshelf. Choosing God's Best! The book Megan gave me shortly before my trip to Romania! I grabbed it and flung it open to any page.

A Prescription for Failure.

I read on, tears quickly forming in my eyes as Dr. Raunkir's words spoke to me as if he were God Himself. This is exactly what's happened between Jonathan and me:

building up all the physical and emotional, not really the friendship and spiritual.

Fifteen pages later and cheeks damp from tears, I arrived at the final paragraph of the chapter:

God's plan for biblically based, healthy, healing relationships is courtship. You can avoid the lifelong heartache and disappointment of dating by focusing on Christ, making proper courtship preparations, and having a spiritual couple who can hold you accountable. If you are already in a dating relationship or think you have gone too far in the other direction, understanding the courtship process will teach you how to receive healing as God restores 'the years the locusts have eaten' (Joel 2:25). Hang tight and remember that the greater the devastation, the greater the restoration.

My cell phone rang. I scrambled off my bed and snatched it from my dresser: *My Dream Boy.*

Oh my gosh! What crazy-perfect timing!

Heart wild, I swiftly answered. "Hello?"

"Hey." Jonathan sounded glummer than the night he serenaded me, likely due to the fact that it's been day three, and I still haven't called him saying I've decided to get back with him.

I plunked onto my bed and opened the book. "I have to read something to you."

"Okay."

I reread the entire chapter to him, not missing a single word on the fifteen pages of mic-drop wisdom. Jonathan listened so intently and quietly, I had to check the phone a couple of times to ensure he hadn't hung up on me. Heart picking up again, I closed the book. "And right when I finished reading that, you called!"

Jonathan hesitated before answering. "Okay…?"

"I think God wants us to court. I even spoke to Pastor John about being our spiritual father when I was in Romania."

"What's courting and what's a spiritual father?"

Strength and vigor returned to my limbs as renewed hope brought life back to my bones. "Courtship is very different from dating. You are not physical at all in the beginning, you're just building up the friendship and then you build a spiritual foundation—serve together, go to church together. The physical comes last and there are boundaries. It's basically a process that prepares you for marriage. And a spiritual father is a godly man who looks over your relationship from the outside and points out things you may not see, gives you advice etcetera."

My heart pounded as I waited for Jonathan to respond, his silence swiftly beginning to drown out my hope of getting back together. Will he be willing to court me? Or is it really over between us?

"But you really hurt me." He broke the silence with an unpromising tone. "I'm not sure I wanna be with you."

I winced. I was afraid of that. Putting the phone on mute, I closed my eyes and began to pray. "God, if you don't want us together, harden his heart against me. But if you do want us back together, to start again —the right way—then let Jonathan forgive me. Let him take me back." I opened my eyes and took the phone off mute as yet more moments of silence elapsed. Shoulders tense, I braced myself for what could be goodbye to this special young man I'd dreamed about four months ago. I'm prepared for whatever it is God wants, no matter how much it hurts.

"I wanna grow old with you, Natasha." Jonathan's confession brought a soothing peace that relaxed my shoulders. "But I think we should take things slow, be like friends—no kissing or anything. But we don't get to know anyone else."

I broke into a smile. "Deal."

"All right." Jonathan's voice also sounded less tense, but still reserved. I get it, I'd be guarded as well if he'd dumped me out of the blue for a few days and blamed it on God. His girlfriend came back from Romania even more radical and spiritual than when she left. "Wanna come to my church's youth group with me at 7:30?" Jonathan asked.

"Sure."

"Okay. I'll be there around seven."

Joy and relief bubbled inside me as we said our goodbyes. My cheeks hurt as I hung up and collapsed onto my pillows. The friendship aspect of our relationship is exactly what I want to build. Now I know we're off to a good start—a new and right beginning. And who knows, maybe this Wednesday he can meet Pastor John and we'll officially have a spiritual father…

I laughed as I peered up at my ceiling. "I guess he is the one."

***

Churchgoers of all colors, shapes, and sizes crowded the main corridor outside the vast sanctuary: the aftermath of the Wednesday night 6:30 service. Talk about Where's Waldo?

I looked around the horde for Pastor John, clenching my Bible as Jonathan stood at my side, waiting patiently—and beautifully—in a white shirt, so crisp against his raven-colored waves and sharp green eyes. Although, without all the kisses and hugs, the swoons hadn't been so give-me-raisin-cakes weakening. "I can't believe I didn't get his cell number or at least plan where we'd meet. That wasn't very smart of me."

"It's okay," Jonathan said. "Maybe he's outside the office."

"Yeah, I guess that's possi"—the assistant pastor, Miguel, stood across the bathrooms, wiping off his black-rimmed glasses as he conversed with a few middle-aged men. "Look, it's Pastor Miguel! Maybe he'd know where Pastor John is." I scurried over to the short Mexican and interrupted one of the men mid-sentence. "Excuse me, sorry. Pastor Miguel, I just wanted to know if you knew where Pastor John is."

Miguel put his glasses on. "He's probably heading over to the radio station. He does a Celebrate Recovery show on Wednesday nights. If the buses haven't left yet, you can catch him at the south side of the building."

"Thanks, Pastor Miguel!" I grabbed Jonathan's hand and darted outside as one of the old deacons Jonathan and I prayed with a couple times pulled out of a parking space. The windows of his blue minivan were down. "Babe, it's Charlie! I bet he knows where the buses are." I ran over to him before he could drive off. "Hey, Charlie."

His eyes—wrinkly with wisdom—glistened behind his rimless glasses. "Natasha, Jonathan, how can I help you all?"

"We're trying to catch Pastor John before he goes to the station," I said, "but we don't know where the buses are that pick him up."

"Oh, I know where they go. Hop in and I'll drive you guys over there."

"Ahh! Thanks so much!"

The door slid open of its own accord and Jonathan and I hopped into the minivan carriage.

"How've you two been?" Charlie asked as he chauffeured us behind the church.

"We've been good." I glimpsed at Jonathan to ensure he'd shared my sentiment. The breakup was still quite recent...Jonathan smiled cordially. My stomach tightened. Was he just being politically correct because we were on church grounds?

"That's great." Charlie went on, all glossy-eyed like a proud grandpa. "I've been praying for you guys."

Jonathan laid his own shiny eyes on me, his gorgeous face bright with obvious joy now. "Thank you."

Butterflies flapped in my belly as I smiled back at him. "Thank you, Charlie."

"Not at all. That's just what I'm supposed to do."

I looked at my little pink Precious Moments Bible in my lap. Good old Charlie's right. Prayer is something all Christians are called to do. And my goodness am I thankful for the ones who take the time to. They really make a difference. God's been apparently answering Charlie's prayers regarding me and Jonathan…

The kind deacon parked the van beside the back entrance where one white bus sat. "Well, here you are. You two be good now."

The butterflies in my stomach morphed into bees, buzzing around in rapid excitement as we said our goodbyes and jumped out of Charlie's van. I strode at a swift pace toward the bus. Mom would have a heart failure at the way I'd carried myself the last five minutes, calling me Desperate Daisy or Desperation Nation, but time is of the essence, and all the big names in the Bible always seemed to obey God with a sense of urgency. If God is telling me to do something, why should I sit around and dawdle? In moments Jonathan's going to meet the man that God has chosen to be our spiritual father. In moments we're going to be one large step closer to preparing for marriage.

My adrenaline screeched to a stop as we reached the bus—devoid of people.

We're too late.

I frowned as I turned to Jonathan, my hopes of finding Pastor John now emptier than the bus. "I guess he's not here. Maybe tonight it just wasn't meant to be." As much as I hate to admit it, this all did seem a bit forced...on my end, what with all the running around like a pig fleeing a Cuban butcher. Worst of all, Jonathan didn't appear super excited to meet Pastor John when I told him about it. Maybe God doesn't want this to happen yet for some reason, or maybe Jonathan isn't ready...

"Don't just give up." Jonathan took out his car keys. "Let's go to the station."

I eyed him. Okay, maybe he is ready.

"Come on, you give up too easily." He jogged ahead of me to the barren parking lot. "Do you know where the station is?"

"Yes." I ran to keep up with him. Maybe he's even more ready than I previously thought. Has he been watching YouTube videos on courtship or something? Or better yet, has this whole courting thing got him thinking about marriage? Or maybe because he's an actor and I've been acting like a crazed spy on a world-ending mission, he's just playing off my performance. We did enjoy role-playing out of nowhere together.

But if he actually is ready…I grinned as we reached his Honda and hopped inside. Then maybe waiting five or six years is starting to make as little sense to him as it did to me the night he shared the terrible idea.

Like Blade's sidekick, Whistler, I directed Jonathan to the radio station headquarters, just north of the church's building. He parked the car and hastily got out, now really behaving like the lead in a Tom Cruise movie.

I bustled after him as he strode through the deserted parking lot toward the beige building.

"There isn't anyone out here," I said.

"Come on." Jonathan trotted up to a back exit and pulled on the handle. "It's locked. Maybe there's another way to get in."

I smiled at his now extremely encouraging determination, though my heart began to deflate. "I love your enthusiasm, but I think it's not meant to happen tonight."

Jonathan sighed as he released the handle. "At least we tried."

"Yeah." I looked up at the moon as we walked back to the car. In Your timing, Lord, not mine.

16. UNCERTAINTY

Will Jonathan ever come back to church with me again? I studied his face as we sat on the living room couch, the house uncomfortably silent now that my family went to sleep.

His forehead creased in contemplation, his back hunched as he gazed ahead with elbows on knees, clearly avoiding my stare.

"What did you think about the pastor's message tonight?" I said quietly.

"I mean, I'd have to research the claim that the belief of the Eucharist becoming the literal blood and body of Christ when consumed, came from a rivalry between two popes trying to say they were the true pope."

I treaded very lightly, my heart thumping heavily. "What if it's true?"

"I don't know if it is yet." Jonathan's deep eyes landed on mine. "I do agree with him though, when he said we need to know why we believe what we believe, because the what produces the how we live it out."

"I agree with that, too." My gaze wandered to the portrait behind us on the wall of Mom and Dad with their big 80s hair, standing at the altar holding hands. "When I was little, and sort of raised Catholic, I would proclaim to be Catholic, but my reason was, 'because my parents are.' It wasn't like I truly knew or understood why the Catholic Church did certain things and why I believed in it. I just did. But now—when I compare Catholic traditions to the Bible—I find that many of them aren't even in the Bible, and if anything, they tend to undermine it."

Jonathan's eyebrow rose. "How so?"

I proceeded with more caution. "Well, Catholicism can be very…ritualistic. Kneel, sit, stand, kneel. Whereas, in the Bible, God and the way believers relate to Him is very relational. You don't find formulas like 'pray the rosary twenty-five times to be forgiven,' or, 'confess to a priest.' What you actually find is Jesus saying the opposite: 'When you pray, do not use vain repetitions like the pagans do. For they think their prayers are answered merely by repeating their words again and again.' Actually, according to the law—which was in the Old Testament for the Jews—they needed to go to a high priest who would offer a sacrifice to God on their behalf in order to be forgiven. But now the Bible says in the New Testament, in Hebrews, 'The oath, which came after the law, appointed the Son who has been made perfect forever, who intercedes on our behalf.' We're under grace now, not the law, so we don't have to go to a priest. We can just go straight to God through Jesus because He's our priest now."

Jonathan sat up, shoulders squared like he'd done before when ready to have a verbal brawl. "I think the fact that they kneel before God shows their respect for Him."

My own tone now tensed. "Yeah, but it's not a requirement. And if they're doing it without acknowledging why, then they're doing it in vain."

"Well, when I have kids I wanna take them to Catholic and Non-denominational Christian church and let them choose what they want to be."

I gulped, crippling fear and a flood of doubt rapidly invading my heart. I completely disagree. I believe the kids would be confused and divided. And if Mommy and Daddy are divisive, they would begin to question why, and I would be totally honest with my answers: I don't go to Catholic Church because I don't agree with its man-made, extra biblical doctrines. And that would cause problems between Jonathan and me. *And the two will become one.* I'm pretty sure that means one in everything, especially in theistic views which we both believe is the foundation for everything else.

I peered at Jonathan, my doubts becoming more and more unsettling.

Are we really made for each other?

***

One of the worst things in life is uncertainty. Which college should I go to? What career should I pursue? Why was I born? What's my purpose in life? Thankfully, I know the answer to all of those inquiries, but there's still one really big one I'm not sure about…

I slid off my bed and onto my knees, the question that'd been haunting me ever since Jonathan and I got back together now in the forefront of my mind. "God, please reveal to me if Jonathan is the man You've chosen for me to be with. I need to know. Speak to me through Your Word please. In Jesus' name. Amen." Sharp pains pierced my heart, instantly bringing tears to my eyes. Weeping as the pain increased, I snatched my Bible off the bed and opened it to anything.

I will make a pathway through the wilderness. I will create rivers in the dry wasteland. Isaiah 43:19

I stared at the page. I don't get it.

Read it in the Amplified.

I looked to my right. My Amplified Bible lay conveniently on the night table, as if placed there purposefully. I snatched it and reopened to Isaiah 43:19.

Behold, I am doing a new thing! Now it springs forth; do you not perceive and know it and will you not give heed to it? I will even make a way in the wilderness and rivers in the desert. The beasts of the field honor Me, the jackals and the ostriches, because I give waters in the wilderness and rivers in the desert, to give drink to My people, My chosen. The people I formed for Myself that they may set forth My praise [and they shall do it].

I blinked a few times as my crying came to an end. I know in the Bible the Word of God is likened to water, and that Jesus Himself is God's Word made flesh, and He says those who drink of Him will never thirst again, that He'll create, 'fountains of living water,' inside the person who believes in Him.

My heart pounded in coordination with my thoughts. So then You're saying that someday Jonathan is going to be filled with

You and Your Word, and that he will live for You? And, 'My chosen'? That must mean...

The all-consuming fire of God's faithfully relentless love melted every ounce of my pain away. Tears of gratitude replaced those of sorrow as I breathed in His peace and His presence. Though I don't know how, or when, I believe now that these verses will be made true in Jonathan's life someday, and that I'll be around to witness it.

I rested a hand over my now steadily beating heart. "Thank You for answering me, Father."

***

I should really get rid of my Facebook. I glanced over my shoulder at Natalia's open bedroom door. The hallway remained unoccupied. I returned to the white and blue homepage of the infamously addicting website. I spend way too much time on this thing, and admittedly, the bulk of it is wasted on snooping around Jonathan's page reading comments from fifis who probably like him. This whole jealousy thing is becoming somewhat of a problem...

A notification popped up at the bottom of the screen.

Eliza Rodriguez wants to be your friend.

Eliza? My sister's ex-best-friend from high school's little sister Eliza? I clicked on her name.

For am I now trying to win the favor of people, or God? If I were still trying to please people, I would not be a servant of Christ. -Galatians 1:10

I clicked on her picture to make sure this was the right Eliza. Long, curly brown hair, latte colored Brazilian skin, and a beautiful, now braces-free smile. Yup, this is her. I can't believe she's a Christian now. That's so awesome! I got another sister in Christ, woot woot!

I quickly accepted the request and then wrote her a message.

Hey, Eliza! How have you been? I see you're a Christian now! That's awesome. Text me sometime!

I typed in my number and hit send. It's amazing…I never knew Eliza very well—I sort of hung out with her a couple of times when I went with my sister to her house—but I know she wasn't a Christian, and now that she is one, she randomly comes back into my life. It's crazy how I went from being completely alone in my faith, with all the people that were closest to me—except my dad—thinking I was insane, to now having all these girls placed in my path who love Jesus just as much as I do. And what's even more incredible is how my family is warming up to the idea.

The fact that Mom started going back to church regularly with Dad and doesn't stare at me with wide eyes anymore is a miracle. Natalia I have to continue praying for. All the coming home late and partying... Although I still rejoiced over her accepting the Bible I got her for her birthday a few months ago.

I logged out of Facebook and grabbed my cell off the desk, my wrists tingling. I think I'm just gonna fast from the computer or something—four hours is apparently too much.

My phone vibrated as I trotted downstairs and into the kitchen. New text message:

Hey, Natasha! It's Eliza. I just got your Facebook message. How are you?

I hopped into a chair by the island. Dang she got it fast. She must get text alerts or something.

I'm great, girl. How have you been?

I've been blessed. God is so good! My boyfriend and I just got engaged and there was a moment where we almost broke up.

I frowned as I texted back. I can relate to that, but thankfully my breakup was actually for the good.

Can I ask why?

A couple of minutes passed. I decided to get some cookies while I waited for her to respond. Hopefully I didn't cross a line; I know we don't know each other very well, but I mean she is the one who brought up the whole breakup thing. I'm just curious as to why it almost came to that and how they worked it out. It's not like I'm gonna go and spread it around to everyone.

The front door burst open. Natalia, eyes red, marched inside with her phone to her ear. She dropped her purse. As many of its contents scattered across the floor a slew of cuss words followed. "Yeah, nothing, I just dropped my stuff," she said to whoever listened on the line.

I hurried over and helped her. I picked up a white paper—a speeding ticket. Nati snatched it from my hand. "I got it, thanks." After rapidly collecting the remainder of her fallen items, she stomped up the stairs toward her bedroom, phone still to her ear. "Yeah, and he found weed on me, too." She slammed her bedroom door.

I flinched at the force. I remember her teenage years. She'd had a number of outbursts, like that time she flung a full water bottle at my head, but now, they seemed even more intense, and this had been what, her fourth speeding ticket since she'd moved back in? And apparently, the cop found marijuana on her. What would her punishment be…?

My phone vibrated as I sat in the chair again. Eliza finally responded to my question.

Well, I used to be very Catholic. I was the only one in my family who would go to mass on Sunday, and Brian was a Christian. He'd invite me to his church, but when I went I felt uncomfortable. It was very different from my church. So I stopped going and we would sometimes argue about it because I believed in God, but I didn't have that relationship I saw Brian had.

I reread Eliza's words. Okay, this all sounds freakishly familiar.

One day, we got into a big fight and were about to break up, but we watched Fireproof together—

Fireproof? The movie I saw with Jonathan?

—and then prayed about it, and Brian was like, 'I never knew a girl like you and with your faith. I don't want us to break up.' And a couple of months later, my cousin invited me to her nondenominational church, and I liked it. I started going to hers and reading the Bible, and I just fell in love with God, and now I'm a Christian and engaged!

I put the phone down on the island counter. Okay, what are the chances that when Eliza gets in touch with me she's a Christian who used to be Catholic and was dating a Christian who she had some problems with because of their differing beliefs and almost broke up, but then watched Fireproof and got back together? It's like she's Jonathan and I'm Brian…

Is this a sign or something? Will this happen with me and Jonathan if I just shut up and pray for him? I picked up the phone again. *Wow, I'm going through the same thing! My boyfriend is Catholic and stopped going to church with me, and he doesn't really read the Bible, and I feel like he's lacking relationship with God, and I've been doubting if I should be with him or not.*

Just keep praying for him and being a light to him. He'll come around.

A familiar peace rested upon my heart, covering my fears and doubts—the peace I felt the night Jonathan and I met for the first time in person as we sat in my living room and held hands.

I smiled as I looked at Eliza's text. "Okay God. That's what I'll do."

17. THE MISTAKE

It is seriously difficult not to cry after what I just witnessed. Almost everyone in that church was so not into it. Yawns, nodding out, talking—some even rolling their eyes! I've never seen a Confirmation, but now that I know what it is, and witnessed how the people getting 'confirmed' reacted to it, how can my heart not break for them?

I battled tears as Jonathan and I walked to his car, night stretching over the church building, gray and dull like many of its congregants. From what I gathered, Confirmation is basically going through various classes and studying certain areas of the Bible alongside Catholicism, and when you're done you have a ceremony, and a bishop or priest ordains you as 'confirmed,' meaning you have, 'become more firmly united to Christ,' and 'received special strength of the Holy Spirit to spread and defend the faith by word and action,' and that now your baptism has been 'perfected.'

Disappointment mingled with my sadness as we got into Jonathan's car. Nowhere in the Bible is such a system found. Not even the word 'confirmation.' According to the Bible I read, there isn't a formula to receive certain things from God, but you just draw near to Him, spend time with Him, love Him, and you'll grow naturally.

Our drive to the outdoor mall was accomplished in complete silence. But I couldn't bring myself to speak—yet.

Jonathan turned to me as we parked in front of the romantically lit shops, bustling with people on this otherwise lovely Saturday evening. "What's wrong?"

"I don't wanna talk about it now." I stepped out of the car.

He strode after me. "Natasha, I saw you crying during mass."

I slowed my pace. I should have known he did. I wasn't trying very hard to conceal my tears because I was so broken for the people getting confirmed. Well, I guess now that he saw me, I might as well confess all. "It's just the people seemed so disconnected. It's like, obviously they want to have a relationship with God, but what they're really getting is a relationship with the Catholic Church."

Jonathan gawped at me like I'd just slapped him in the jaw. "Are you serious right now? How do you know what their relationship with God is like? Wow, Natasha. Just don't come with me anymore if all you're going to do is cry when you go. It's really rude of you!"

A few passersby looked back at us as we stopped outside the doors of our favorite Chinese restaurant.

My blood temperature rose—as did my voice. "I just care for them. They probably go to church every Sunday and then go about their lives, totally missing that faith in Christ isn't a one day a week church mass. It's accepting you've messed up—that you're not perfect, but that Jesus is. Church attendance doesn't equal heaven or a relationship with God. He's so much more intimate than that. He wants our love, our hearts."

Jonathan smacked his thighs. "Man, Natasha, you think because everyone's not like you they're not going to heaven?"

I held my tongue. I'm not going to do this right now. I'm not going to fight with him in front of an audience. I turned around, walking as fast as I could. I tore into a Barnes and Noble, my heart pounding harder as I ran past aisles of books, an exit door a few yards beyond me. I slammed it open and strode back outside, this time in a different part of the mall. A Mexican restaurant neighbored the bookstore. I strode inside and made my way to a table in the very back, my ears ringing from the rush of blood flooding my head.

I can't believe the way Jonathan snapped on me. He doesn't get it. He's so stuck in his religion and tradition that he can't even see that it's not making that big of a difference in his life because God isn't the Catholic Church, He's God. I took my phone out of my purse. I just wanna go home, but not with him.

Dace. A voice spoke in my mind, clear and definitive.

I looked around the restaurant, desolate apart from the employees. Dace? But I can't.

Don't. A quieter voice said.

Why not?

Because Jonathan wouldn't be very happy about that.

So? Look at how he treated you, and in front of others.

That's true. And it's not like I'm going to cheat on him or anything. I'll just ask Dace if he can pick me up so my mom doesn't have to know Jonathan and I got into a fight.

I pressed the home button on my phone. The screen remained black. Freak, it's dead.

A greasy haired kid likely my age worked behind the food counter.

I approached him. "Excuse me, can I use your phone? Mine died."

"Sure." He picked up a cordless phone from the counter and handed it to me.

"Thank you." I dialed Dace's number as I sat at the table again, a small tremble making its way through my limbs.

Don't do—

"Hello?"

Sweat moistened my palms. "Hi, Dace. It's Natasha. Are you busy?"

"Not at the moment…"

"Can you do me a huge favor?" Sweat seeped out of my forehead and the trembling worsened. "Can you pick me up?"

"Something told me you were going to call me tonight." He sounded amused, impressed even. "Where are you?"

I ignored the hair beginning to rise on the back of my neck. "I'm at Lime in the shops at Pembroke Gardens."

"Okay, I'll look it up on my GPS. I'll be there in twenty minutes."

"Okay, bye."

"Bye, Natasha."

My hands shook hard as I hung up. What did I just do?

Don't worry about it now.

I glimpsed outside. My heart skipped. Across the street, Jonathan strode past stores, looking around frantically. I ducked my head. Gosh, why am I doing this? He's probably so worried about me. I should at least tell him I'm okay.

I began dialing his number on the cordless. Dang it, I can't remember the order of the last four digits. Is it 5295 or 5995? I think it's 5995.

"Your call has been forwarded to an automatic voice messaging system."

Great. His phone must have died as well.

Beep.

I spoke into the receiver. "It's me. I just wanted to let you know that I'm okay. I got a ride home so don't worry about me. I'll text you when I'm there." I paused, the three words I usually say before goodbye clogged in my throat. "Bye, Jonathan."

I gathered the strength to stand and returned the phone to the young man before slumping back to the table. This night was horrible. Me and Jonathan never raised our voices like that at each other. Sure he was upset when we broke up and he came to my house, but not like this. How can we be right for each other if he's so passionate about his views on what a relationship with God looks like, and mine are so different? It's not something we can 'agree to disagree' on. It's too important.

I gazed outside to where I saw Jonathan searching for me. But what about those verses, Isaiah 43:19-21? And what I read in Choosing God's Best? And then the text conversation I had with Eliza. That didn't seem coincidental. I mean me and Jonathan both believe Jesus is the Son of God, but I'm just not for making God a religion. Even the apostle Paul said God doesn't live in man-made temples, and human hands can't serve His needs, because He doesn't have any. I wish Jonathan knew these things. If only he read the Bible himself. Maybe then he'd see it's not my opinion, it's just what the Word of God says.

Dace's black Altima pulled into view, blocking out where I last saw Jonathan. I put my dead cell back in my purse as I arose shakily to my feet. Here we go.

I scanned the area as I scurried outside and into his car, Jonathan thankfully nowhere in sight.

"Hello." Dace's dark brown hair fell in flat wisps against his pale cheeks, two fanglike lip rings jutting from both ends of his bottom lip.

I purposed to speak as professionally as possible. "Thank you for coming."

"I said I couldn't always be there for you, but that I'd try my best." He peered at me, his eyes dark, but not as dark as they have been in the past...

I looked away as he drove off. "How have you been?"

"I've been...alive." He chuckled. "Someone shot at me so I fled to North Carolina for a few weeks."

As I gawked at him, Dace's grin widened. "I don't know why those bastards want me dead so bad."

"Well...um..."

"You made your hair blonder."

"Yeah." I eyed him, a smirk still curving the right side of his mouth up. I guess changing the subject is a good thing. I don't think I want to know the drama he's gotten himself into now. "You planning on getting any more piercings?"

"The industrial." He glanced at me, his smile fading. "Why'd you call me?"

"I don't know. Me and Jonathan..." I stared out the window and watched the passing street lamps. "We got into an argument."

"I figured as much. May I ask why?"

I pressed my back against my chair as we stopped at a red light, a silver Honda on our left. Please don't let it be Jonathan, please don't let it be Jonathan.

Dace followed my stare. He glimpsed at me as the light turned green and then sped up as he merged onto the highway.

I sat upright again. My shaking gradually subsided the farther we got from the Honda. Should I tell him about the greatest issue in me and Jonathan's relationship? Dace did pull that whole messaging stunt. I mean, he seems a little different, lighter somehow. Maybe my prayers for him have been working…?

"Jonathan's Catholic," I finally said, "so we butt heads sometimes."

"Ah," Dace gave a nod. "The Catholic Church is…interesting."

"Yeah. We just view things differently. Like the importance of reading the Bible."

"I have to start reading again. I've been going back to church though." Dace offered another quick look before saying, "Even August goes with me now."

I continued my professionalism, not surprised he decided to go back to the "more of a fighter" girl he lost his virginity to.

"You're going to church again? That's good. And I'm glad August goes."

"Yeah. She's kind of angry at God, but she's getting there."

I sighed. It stinks when God gets all the blame for every tragedy or bad thing that happens to a person, as if Satan doesn't exist or people's own choices don't sometimes have consequences. "I'll pray for her."

"Thank you."

I watched the highway lights once more as we sat in silence for a while, no longer feeling as awkward and jittery. Dace and I definitely messed up with how physical we were, but I can't deny that we shared a friendship—unlike all my previous exes besides that one Frenchy. And even though he's hurt me a lot with things he's said and done, he has been there for me many times. I almost wish we never crossed those boundaries and just remained friends.

But I didn't know any better, so I just let my emotions and my own selfish desires get the best of me. No, the worst of me, and that brought out the worst in him. But as much as I want to rectify my past sins, I can't go back in time. I messed up, and now one of the many consequences of my actions is a severed friendship that can never be restored. At least not here on earth.

"Are you going to tell him I was the one who picked you up?" Dace's question sent chills down my spine.

"Well, yeah, although honestly, I'm kind of dreading it."

"Do you think he'll break up with you?"

I winced. "I don't know." Gosh, I sure hope not. I didn't even think of what the repercussions of all this would be. Jonathan did say he wanted to punch Dace in the face the last time they had their first and only real conversation. Now he's going to find out the same ex who said terrible things about me is the person I decided to make my getaway driver after things hit the fan. I rubbed my temples. Gosh, this was a terrible mistake.

"Well." Dace's voice also turned professional. "I've already told August. She's not very enthused by the idea, but I told her that if you and I were going to be friends, she has to trust me and that there'll be boundaries. For instance *this*, won't happen again."

"Yeah…" I stopped rubbing my pounding temples. "I don't think us being friends will fly well with Jonathan, and I can understand why, so I really don't think *this* will happen again."

"What if you asked him?" Dace's eyes briefly locked onto mine before looking back at the road.

"He wouldn't be 'enthused.'" And neither would I.

We pulled up to my house.

Dace gazed at me. No glimmer lightened his eyes. His dark stare returned and reminded me of the look he gave me that February 22nd night before walking off my porch, when we both sacrificed our relationship for good. "I guess this is goodbye then."

"I believe so," I said.

He gave a gentle nod. "If you ever need me, I'm here."

"Thank you." I stepped out of the car.

"Good luck."

"Thanks." I closed the door and walked to my house. I can't do this again. This will be the last time I call on Dace, and terrifyingly, tomorrow might be the last time Jonathan calls me.

***

Trembling, I opened my front door and stepped outside into the sun's spotlight. The main street across from my house buzzed with several cars, though Sunday's were always slightly more chill than weekdays, but one car sat parked on my driveway—Jonathan's silver Honda.

As I approached, the driver's side door opened. Jonathan stepped out, all bright and saintly in a white v-neck, but his green eyes carried a darkness to them, anger...

I halted before him and squeaked, "Hi."

"Hey."

"I'm...really sorry I ran away from you last night."

"Yeah that was messed up."

My heart kicked up several gears. Messed up. Yeah. It totally was. But what's he gonna think when he finds out how freaking extra messed up by summoning a blast from the past.

"I never would've thought you'd run away from me and hide," Jonathan's voice shook. "I thought you got kidnapped."

"I know, my dad told me you called Nati and that they were on the way to find me, but I called before they got there."

"And I called my dad who came and helped me look for you. And I was about to call the police, but I called your sister first and I told her that I thought you were kidnapped, and she started crying. I looked everywhere for you for hours."

Heart now bleeding like the red driveway we both stood on, I couldn't hold the truth in any longer. "I…called Dace to pick me up."

Jonathan froze as if the White Witch from Narnia turned him to stone. After several moments of shocked staring at me, his stupid girlfriend, he finally broke from his trance and shifted his view to the loud cars whizzing by.

He puckered his lips before saying, "I thought you were better than that."

His words hit my chest and tears slipped from eyes. "Nothing happened, we didn't touch or anything, and I told him I wouldn't be calling again."

"Until the next fight."

"No, I really don't plan on it. I just, I don't know, was attacked or something at a very opportune moment."

Jonathan gave slow nods. "You were attacked? Like he came and kidnapped you and held you captive?"

"No, not attacked by him, attacked by Satan or his demons." I rubbed my arms where goosebumps rode. "As I sat there after leaving you a voicemail, this voice came into my head saying to call Dace, and now that I think about it, it didn't seem like mine—or God's."

"But you listened to it."

"Yes, and that was weak and stupid of me."

Jonathan about faced me. "I was worrying my heart out while you were hanging out with your ex."

"I wasn't hanging out with him. He gave me a ride home and that was it, I promise." More tears leaked from eyes. "Please forgive me."

As Jonathan's gaze lifted up to the sky. I smacked my head. I did one of the worst things you can do in a relationship: betray the trust. All because I let my emotions get the best of me and ignored God's warning. If I keep doing this, I'm gonna completely destroy our relationship! I have to earn his trust back. Please Lord, Your Word says You work all things together for the good of those who love You. Somehow, get him to trust me again. Please!

Jonathan surveyed me. His shoulders relaxed—some. "I will, but I think I need a few days."

I sighed, my heart-rate gradually slowing, and leaned against his car. "Thank you." The words I failed to tell him last night on the voicemail burned in my throat. "I love you, Jonathan."

His eyes shimmered as he peered up at me, his beautiful face downcast. "I should go."

I nodded, pain pouncing over my heart all over again. I stepped away from his car and watched as he got inside and then drove off.

18. WORK IN PROGRESS

Twilight stretched above the Universal Studios parking lot I skipped through, Jonathan behind me. I peeked over my shoulder at him. His beautiful form melded with the melodies still playing in my head from the concert that day. *"I've made a mess of me, I wanna reverse this tragedy. I've made a mess of me, I wanna spend the rest of my life alive!"*

Jonathan's eyes glowed as they followed me. Now mom's words rode over Switchfoot's song: *"You guys are like, mesmerized by each other."*

I'd surely made a mess of myself and created a tragedy that desperately needed reversing. But I couldn't reverse it. I couldn't go back and undo what I'd so foolishly done.

Jonathan called me a few days ago, after taking a little bit of a breather from me, and divulged on an experience he had. Before my dreadful confession the following afternoon, I'd briefly got in touch with Jonathan the night of the Dace debacle, and let him know I was alive. We hung up, but wrath had captured Jonathan's heart. He thanked God I was all right, but felt like he didn't even want to forgive me. He turned the TV on and happened across a pastor giving a sermon. The man's words jumped out of the screen and into Jonathan's heart. He couldn't remember exactly what the pastor was saying, but he knows what God was saying through him. "It seemed like a gentle wrestling match with God," Jonathan told me over the phone, "like he was saying, 'I don't want you to hold onto this, I want you to let it go. You know the right thing to do.' And it was becoming more uncomfortable to hold onto the anger. Slowly, I came to my senses and knew that God wanted me to forgive you. I also felt like God had answered my prayer in keeping you safe. And how could I be unforgiving when God answered me and you were okay?"

I'd clenched the phone, still wondering if he was going to dump me or not, since that experience happened *before* I dropped the atomic ex-bomb on him.

Jonathan continued. "I didn't like what you did with your ex, but I still felt that same sense that God wanted me to forgive you, like I had the other night."

And forgive he did. I'd literally been praying to go to a Christian concert and to a theme park, and I managed to be a winning caller over the radio for two tickets to Rock the Universe—and Jonathan agreed to go with me.

"That was so awesome!" I said as we reached Jonathan's car.

He opened the door for me, a lovely chuckle easing from his beautiful lips—that still taunted at times, although less fiercely. "It was a good time. I think I liked Jeremy Camp the best."

"He was really good. I love how every artist we watched shared something personal with the audience. It made it so much more special. Like you were able to connect even more with them and praise God for how He inspired their songs."

"It was really cool. Definitely encouraging."

My heart simmered with joy as we drove away from the theme park. Little by little, Jonathan has been getting closer to God. I remember he always had secular music on in his car and so, without saying anything to him about it, I just prayed behind his back like Eliza told me to. Now every time I'm in his car, it's on a Christian radio station. With all these answered prayers—and attacks— maybe he really is the one God had tucked away for me all along…

I reclined the passenger seat. "You looked traumatized during Pillar's songs."

"I was."

I backhanded his arm. "Oh come on, they're so fun!"

"Yeah…I just can't get behind that one. It's like ear torture."

"Psh! I love music that pumps you up!"

Jonathan stole a glance. "It's a good thing you're so pretty."

"What's that supposed to mean?"

"I wouldn't let just any girl torture me."

I unleashed a boisterous laugh. Goodness, that boy's got lines for days.

Jonathan smiled as he took my hand. "You're not just my girlfriend, you're my best friend."

"Seriously?"

"Yeah."

My heart jumped as I turned toward him. Oh my gosh, I prayed that we would someday become best friends! Can this trip get any better?

Jonathan stole another look. "So I know this trip was supposed to end here, but…I planned something special for you."

"Aww, Jonathan! You didn't have to."

"Are you ready for one more adventure this weekend?"

I stared at him in disbelief. I guess this day can get better! Goodness, this is amazing, but what's even more amazing is the fact that I don't even deserve all this— winning tickets to come to the Rock the Universe concert; Jonathan forgiving me for catching a ride with Dace; telling me I'm his best friend, and now surprising me by taking me to some destination that's probably gonna be awesome. God's mercy on me through all of this has been almost too good to be true.

The night waned on as we recounted our favorite moments of the day; Fireflight really did rock the universe, and Jonathan had actually enjoyed them; the dueling dragons ride had been the best roller coaster, though the Mummy was a close second; and despite being seemingly decades old, the robotic Jaws attraction still felt terrifyingly real.

I glanced at Jonathan, blackness outside the window behind him. Night had crept in two hours ago, and we still hadn't arrived at destination unknown. "So…are we close?"

"I didn't realize it was this far." He frowned as he looked at me. "Maybe we should just do it another time."

"Why don't you call the people and see how far we are." I watched as he dialed a number.

"Hi, I was calling to see where you are located exactly." His brow creased. "Oh, so you have to make a reservation. Can you hold on for a moment?" He held the phone away from his face. "We're close, but I have to make a reservation. They said they're already booked for today. We'd have to do it tomorrow."

My eyes widened. That would mean we'd have to rent a hotel room for a second night. To be real, one night was tempting enough as it is…but a reservation? If this is just a super fancy five-star restaurant or something, I think it's fine if we pass on it.

"Can you tell me what it is?" I said.

Jonathan hesitated.

"I know you wanted it to be a surprise, but I just want to see if it's worth staying overnight for."

"I was gonna take you horseback riding on the beach."

I gaped at him. Great. Why couldn't he say kayaking or something?

"Natasha," Jonathan gently interrupted my trance, "have you ever been horseback riding on the beach?"

Heart sprinting, I welded into my seat. "Make a reservation."

"Are you sure?"

"Yeah."

Jonathan delivered his debilitating smile as he made our reservation. I played with my phone, a sinking feeling in my stomach…

***

I shifted in the full-sized bed. A ray of moonlight slithered into the hotel room through a crack in the curtains. The window air conditioner blew cold air against them and they rustled. Jonathan lay in the other bed, my back toward him. Though I dared not look and darkness swathed us, one thing I knew: my body was searing.

***

Green leaves replaced most of the blue sky canopying Kelly Ranch. Quiet rustles of horses' tails swaying back and forth along with the melodious chirping of the colorful painted buntings soothed my conscience. The beautiful afternoon whispered of God's forgiveness.

I sat beside Jonathan on one of the wooden benches under the trees. "We really can't rent a hotel room when we're alone."

"Yeah." He gazed at me, his hazel eyes filled with determination. "If we ever go on a trip out of town again, we'll take my brother or Natalia, or we won't go."

"Definitely." I looked at the cloudless sky. Temporary pleasure isn't worth hurting God's Spirit, or each other's. Even though I'm still a virgin, going beyond kissing had been such an easy place to land in before I met Jonathan. Heck, I was ready to go for the home run with my previous ex. But now my soul knows whats mine is not mine—it's my Father's, and He tells me it's better to marry than burn with lust. And some days, I feel so strong. I can be around Jonathan and have a blast as besties. But then other days, my brain registers just how freaking swooney he is, and the whole forced proximity thing is like Temptation Island. I love Jesus, but we've gotta conquer this, somehow and soon…

"All right, riders." The owner of the ranch, Hal, looking like one of the nice guys in a cowboy movie, stood beside three horses, two brown and one gray. "We need to cover a few basics before riding." He waited for us to reach him and then started. "When you mount the horse, you gotta make sure your foot is securely in the stirrups." He demonstrated. "Now, with one hand, you hold the reins, and to steer, first give him a gentle kick and then tug slightly to the left if you want 'em to go left, and to the right if you want 'em to go right. And to stop, you just pull back the reins and say 'whoa.' It's real simple. Now let's get saddled up!" He hopped off the horse and then helped me on. "This is Sisqo. He's our youngest horse. And this"—he stroked the mane of the horse behind us as Jonathan mounted it—"is Darla. Now you two remember to steer, you just tug gently."

As Hal saddled the gray horse in front of us, I beamed at my own cowboy, in his plaid button up and jeans, except instead of rocking a hat, he donned a helmet. "Thank you so much for taking me here. I'll never forget this."

"Well, hey, princes are supposed to ride horses right? Let's see if I have what it takes."

"All right, riders," Hal said, "let's go!"

I gently kicked Sisqo's side and he began following Hal onto a small trail surrounded by trees and shrubbery. Beams of light shined through the leaves onto Hal's grayish horse, making him shine like silver. This truly is wonderful. Everything is so beautiful. The ranch, the trees, the hors—We stopped moving. Sisqo feasted on a thick bush.

"If they stop to eat, just kick their side and pull the rein away from the shrubs," Hal called out.

I did so, and Sisqo continued walking. "You're hungry, huh boy?" I looked back at Jonathan. He encountered the same problem with Darla. I laughed as he gently tugged on the rein, Darla happily ignoring his kindly manners. After a few more eaten leaves, the horse finally submitted to his requests.

The trees thinned out and an expanse of white sand and blue sea emerged. The sun reflected off the calm waters, making its smooth surface glitter like diamonds. I peered over my shoulder at Jonathan. His tender smile spoke the three words I love to hear. I sighed as I turned my attention back to the scenery. If earth is this beautiful, I can't imagine what heaven's like; a place with no more sin…no more stumbling…no more wandering and unknowns. No more bitter fighting, and pasts that come back to haunt you, just peace, faith, hope, and love for all eternity.

I breathed in the ocean scent and this memory that I will cherish for as long as I live.

19. SISTER 2.0

Jonathan's face paled, though I'm sure with my stirring blood, mine had to be red. The rowdy laughter of his fellow acting students and the bumping music in the large living room still couldn't drown out Natalia's rising voice. Purse on her arm, a wine-cooler in hand, and her flat stomach exposed, she swayed in front of me like the main hot girl in a rap video. "I told you, I'm fine. I don't need you to drive me home." With every slurred word, my temperature continued to rise.

"Give me your car key, Natalia."

"No, no, I'm fine."

Mauricio, Mr. Tall, Dark, and Handsome Metrosexual she'd been seeing walked beside her. Though he carried a beer, his speech came out much clearer. "It's no big deal, just let your little sister take you."

"I am not going to let you drive my car!" Natalia screamed in my face, causing everyone's focus to zero in on us.

Jonathan took a half-step forward. "Natalia, let's talk outside."

"You know what! You wanna drive!" Natalia ripped her keys from her purse and threw them on the floor. "Go ahead, take them!" She spun around and marched out.

Mauricio's waxed eyebrows jumped before he chugged his beer. "She'll be fine, just let her drive."

Jonathan grabbed the keys. "We can't let Natalia drive home."

"You don't think you're overreacting a bit? She drives home like this all time."

I leered up at her fling. "You're under-reacting, goodbye." I marched outside. The evening hung humid and dark over the landscaped yard. Nati stood by the passenger, arms crossed. Pasco, Nati's number one admirer—according to her and Jonathan—stood in front of her, his tawny face twisted with concern.

As I approached with Jonathan by my side, I planted myself beside Pasco. Jonathan handed me the keys and said, "Your sister's driving."

Natalia turned and slammed her palms against the car. "This is my car! My car! I don't have to let anyone drive it!"

Pasco pouted his fluffy lips. "Please, just tonight, Natalia. And let me know when you get home."

She snorted in a breath before thrusting open the passenger.

Jonathan walked me to the driver's side, his tone tense. "Please do let me know when you're home safe."

"I will." I leaned in and gave him a quick kiss, my hands shaky. As I climbed in, Pasco bent over Natalia, and buckled her seatbelt. He closed the door and Natalia screamed. Profanity streamed from her mouth. She lifted her legs and her boots pummeled the dashboard. The car vibrated with her rage —and perhaps something else.

I set my gaze ahead, Jonathan and Pasco side-by-side, still watching as I slowly pulled out. Lord, please help me stay calm.

"So! Embarrassing!" Nati panted as she rammed her feet back down. Blackened tears lined her cheeks. "This whole thing! I never want you to come to a party with me again! I drive myself home all the time and I'm fine! Fine!"

While I drove us past streetlights, Natalia continued to cuss and shout, even as we got onto the highway. I stared ahead, purposing with every ounce of strength within me to stick out the nearly thirty-minute drive home. Ever since getting caught with marijuana and being forced to attend AA, she'd turned more and more to drinking. God, how is she ever going to give her life to you? She's so full of rage and contempt. She's never hated me this much. And she's also never been this angry and wild before. I knew she liked Mauricio, but did his opinion really matter that much to her? He didn't seem to share the same amount of care, that's for sure. She was just the chick going through a divorce and wanting to have fun in his eyes. And that's what I thought, too. But this isn't fun. This is horrible.

Natalia yelled again and punched the dash. I slammed my foot on the break and turned on the hazards. I stepped out in the middle of the dead highway, and strode to the passenger. Nati had already got out and climbed into the driver's side the same moment I shut the door. She jerked the shift to drive and gunned it. As the speedometer climbed, 45, 65, 80, 90, 100, I breathed in and exhaled, gripping the sides of my seat. Please, God, get us home safe. Please, Lord.

The car hummed and the wind whipped against the windows. I texted Jonathan. *Please pray. I couldn't take her screaming and punching the dash anymore, and felt like she was about to punch me next, so I let her drive. We're on the highway going 100.*

Are you kidding me?! I'm praying!

The time on my phone read 1:02am. I relaxed my grip on the cushion and kept my eyes wide open. Bizarrely, not a single car rode on the highway. Saturday night? Heading toward Miami from Broward?

A peace settled over me as we neared the exit to Mom's house. Although this is stupid dangerous, I don't think God's ready to take either of us just yet. I glimpsed at my big sister, fierce brown eyes ahead. And I really hope He doesn't take her until she's His...

✳✳✳

Four gentle knocks rapped my bedroom door. I ended my midday prayer session, still in my jammies, and opened the door.

Natalia stood before me, also in a big jammy tee and fuzzy pants—and holding the hot pink Bible I got her for her birthday eight months ago. "Can I come in?"

"Of course." I climbed onto my full-sized bed, legs crossed and heart pounding as Nati sat across from me, laying the Bible in her lap. No makeup, her hair in a simple bun, she didn't seem four years older, but four years younger somehow.

Tears welled in her eyes and she exhaled a shaky breath. "Something happened."

Now my heart banged against my chest. It'd been hardly a week since the night she blew up on me. She'd eventually apologized, but nothing seemed to be changing regarding the drinking and partying. But the last few days, she'd been in her room more.

Taking another weary breath, Nati continued. "The other night after a party, I was so sick of who I was. I felt disgusting. I came home and went into Mom and Dad's room...and found Dad's gun." A tear slipped down her cheek.

I gasped and took her hands, both of ours atop the Bible now. "Oh, Nati."

She nodded. "I pressed the barrel in my mouth. I asked God if He was there because I was going to end it. And this voice came into my mind and said, 'There is nothing you can do in this world that's reason enough to pull this trigger.'" More tears escaped and a smile stretched on her beautiful face. "I put the gun down and asked Him to reveal Himself to me. I went in my room and opened the Bible you gave me and started reading Matthew. And I just…" She chuckled, her smile brighter. "Fell in love with Jesus."

Now I cried as I laughed and hugged her. "Oh, Nati! I'm so happy for you! I've prayed so much for you!"

Her embrace felt so soft and gentle, not hard like the strong, gym-attending, ferocious woman who'd been living here the past nine months. It was like holding someone I'd never met before, but yet knew all my life.

I smiled as I pulled away. Yes, her olive skin and chestnut eyes glowed and had softened. This was the real Natalia…the one God had hidden inside of Him like buried treasure. A memory coaxed my mind.

I'd been listening to my favorite Christian radio station, and the host invited listeners to call and request a song. Nati immediately came to mind, along with a song: More Beautiful You, by Johnny Diaz.

The host answered my call, and said she'd play the song next. I quickly dialed Nati. "Turn on this radio station, I made a song dedication to you!"

"Aww, Tashi, that's really sweet, I'll take a listen, thank you."

We'd hung up and after the fact she sent me texts with hearts and crying emojis. And now here she sat, crying in my room, looking more beautiful and clear headed than ever.

"I have this prayer list," I said, "and when I was in Romania, and I got to your name, I would .start praying faster. It happened for a few days and on the third, I actually got the spiritual gift of tongues right after praying for you!"

Her eyes grew and she blinked at me. "Whoa...that's crazy." She caressed my cheek, wiping my tears. "I'm so sorry I was so mean to you. Honestly, you had changed a lot, and it was...convicting. I kinda wanted what you had, but I didn't wanna tell you. I even..." She slowly raised her palm where a silver wedding band with engravings on it wrapped her ring-finger. "...Got a purity ring."

My jaw dropped. I bounced and laughed again, clapping my hands. "I seriously prayed that one day you'd be a purity-ring-wearing, non-cussing, church-attending, Jesus-loving Christian like me!"

"No you didn't!" She joined my laughter. After a few more laughs and hugs, my sweet sister finished with, "Thank you so much, sister, for never giving up on me."

20. NOT COOL

I hurried up the steps to the second story of the theatre building, where my knight-in-shining-armor would be finishing up his new class at any moment. My favorite elf boots clicked against the speckled marble, echoing my presence.

Two girls around my age stood in the hallway, scripts in hand, clearly rehearsing a scene. They stopped and turned to me.

"Hi! I'm just waiting for Jonathan to get out," I said. "I'm his girlfriend."

"Awwww!" One of the girls gestured to an open door. "You can go right in, class is almost over, and our director won't care."

"Thanks so much!" I traversed into the vast room. Several windows at the very back illuminated desks with a large, open space near the front. Many young actors stood by the desks, chatting or acting.

My heart punched my chest. Jonathan leaned against a desk holding a script, Lily—Dace's sister—standing beside him. In a tight crop-top and leggings, every inch of her perfect dancer body flaunted itself.

What the heck is going on here? I moved toward them, sweat beginning to fall down my back. Jonathan gazed up from his script. His marvelous smile somewhat calmed my nerves. "Hey, babe, what are you doing here?"

"Surprising you." I hugged him and turned to Lily. "Good to see you, I didn't know you were into acting." I gave her a genuine hug, though I couldn't help but feel like something about this was off.

"I'm not really, I've just been doing a lot of competitions lately and figured movement for the actor may help the emotional side of my performances."

"That makes sense."

"You dance?" Jonathan said. "That's awesome."

Lily gave her cute fairy smile, her dark eyes shining.

Jonathan set the script down. "How do you two know each other?"

Lily's fairy smile vanished as I decided to throw out the answer. "I dated her brother… Dace."

"Oh…okay."

"Well." I grabbed Jonathan's hand. "It was nice seeing you, Lily."

"You, too. I'm sure we'll see each other more." She hesitated, her eyes glimpsing at Jonathan. "I'm really happy for you guys."

"Thanks," Jonathan answered. "Text me when you wanna get together."

"Yeah, definitely." She waved and I forced myself to walk at a normal pace toward the door.

My insides tumbled around as we walked into the hallway and down the stairs. I tried to keep my tone even while I asked my boyfriend, "Why are you two 'getting together?'"

"Our teacher assigned her as my partner."

"As in, your scene partner?"

Jonathan laughed. "Yeah, what other partner would she be?"

"I don't know," I said as we traversed into the parking lot. "Is it a romantic scene?"

"Not really, but...there is a kiss."

I released Jonathan's hand and halted. "Say what now?"

"Yeah, we're both on this building ledge, and instead of jumping off, we find each other, and the scene ends in a kiss—and us falling off the ledge together. See, not very romantic."

"Your lips touching another girl's mouth, who, by the way, happens to be quite an attractive little pixie, is romantic enough for me."

Jonathan managed to speak in a very unfazed manner. "It's just acting."

I blinked as if gnats harassed my eyeballs. "Just. Acting? It's not acting if your lips are touching, Jonathan."

"Tell that to Stella Adler."

"Tell that to Jesus."

"She's just a scene partner, and I'm not gonna allow myself to grow feelings for her."

"Yeah, because that worked out well with Ember."

"I never had a kissing scene with Ember."

"Yes, which makes it all the more concerning that you're gonna be hanging out with and practicing kisses with my ex's hot sister!"

Jonathan peered over his shoulder. "Do you wanna take this conversation into the car?"

I tromped ahead of him. Is he serious? I don't think he'd appreciate it if my lips were "acting" with a handsome guy.

The moment we sat in his car, I spoke up. "So you're really gonna do this?"

"Everybody else already has a partner. I'm not sure if I can get out of this."

"I guess your career is more important than our relationship."

Jonathan brought on his resoluteness. "It's a scene, I'm an actor. I'll act like she's an old lady with no teeth. Will that make you feel better?"

I looked out the window. No, but slapping him might. I held my tongue. Lord, please help me to trust You to work on Jonathan. Please, God, You're the only One who's never let me down.

✱✱✱

"I feel like it's the enemy." I sat atop my bed, candles burning on my headrest and dresser, illuminating Nati's lovely face, wrinkled in all the right spots with compassion, as she sat with me. Of everyone I know, no one's more compassionate than Natalia. A tear rolled to my chin.

"Oh, sister, it sounds like it." Nati wiped it away. "Sappy isn't perfect, but he loves you, and he's still growing. We all are."

"I know, but he grew feelings for Ember girl in the past, and it's like he's setting himself up again with kissing Lily for this stupid scene."

"Do you know if he's kissed her yet?"

"I don't know. They rehearse together like twice a week."

Nati drew out a sigh. "I'm not gonna lie, I grew feelings for a few of the actors in our old acting class because you know, if they're attractive, and you're spending a lot of time together, and then especially if you're gonna be intimate in any way, it does kinda pull on your heart some."

I smacked my head against a pillow. "See!"

Nati rubbed my back. "Keep praying about it. I believe you guys are made for each other. I swear, I really felt like God wanted you guys to meet."

"But what if Satan can mess that up?"

Eyes glinting in the candlelight, Natalia took my hands off the pillow and into hers. "Sister, we have prayer, and that's stronger than any temptation."

I set the pillow down and nodded. How could I forget that? Nati is living proof of the power of prayer. She tossed her drugs in the devil's face and ran hard after Jesus. I don't know anyone who was praying for her as passionately as I was, and if there's one promise I can cling to, it's that the prayer of the righteous avails much.

I breathed in the peony scented air, rolled my shoulders and declared, "Let's crush Satan beneath our feet."

21. OH HECK NO

I rested my head on Jonathan's shoulder as we sat on my Florida room couch, watching yet another episode of the Tyra Banks show. Mom and Nati chatted in the kitchen, the aroma of the Cinnabons they'd popped in the oven lathering the air. Between their rambunctious chattering and the soon-to-be-devoured dessert, it wasn't a tempting situation. Besides, there were many times I just enjoyed being near to him, enjoyed his friendship—something I'd been praying we would grow more and more in.

Jonathan texted on his phone and then announced, "I gotta go."

I muted the TV. "You don't want to stay for dessert?"

"No, I have a rehearsal."

My hand gripped the remote. "With who?"

Jonathan stood. "With my scene partner."

"At ten o'clock at night?"

"Yeah, we're trying to get as many rehearsals in as we can before our performance next week."

I followed him into the kitchen. "And where do you plan on rehearsing?"

"I gotta go," Jonathan addressed Mom and Natalia. "I'll see you guys later."

"Later, J." As Nati gave him a hug, Mom's chin dipped and her Nancy Drew eyes followed us to the door.

"I'll walk you out," I said and trailed him onto the porch. "You didn't answer my question."

"We're rehearsing at a playground close to her house."

"I don't think it's very appropriate to be rehearsing this late at night."

Jonathan stopped at his car. The streetlight's warm yellow exposed a crease on his brow and a small frown.

M'hmm. I crossed my arms. "So you're gonna go?"

"As soon as you're done interrogating me, officer."

I gave him a dramatic hand clap before stomping back inside. I snatched my phone off of the kitchen counter, where it rested by Nati. What Jonathan doesn't know, is that I actually have Lily's number.

Hi, Lily. I know you and Jonathan have a scene together, but I just don't think it's appropriate to be rehearsing a scene with my boyfriend this late at night. Send.

Natalia peered over my shoulder as Mom ambled over with a cinnabon.

"Oh heck no," Natalia said, gaze on the text I sent.

"What happened?" Mom handed me the bun.

"Oh nothing, just Jonathan thinking he can rehearse with Lily at a playground at ten o'clock at night."

"Isn't that Dace's sister?"

"Yes," me and Nati replied.

"Oh heck no!"

My phone chimed.

Hi, Natasha! You're right, I just texted him and let him know I wanna reschedule. I apologize! Goodnight.

"Thank You, Jesus!" I bit into the sweet, cinnamon-y goodness. "Sometimes you gotta fight for what's yours."

"What happened?" Mom asked.

I handed Nati the phone. After reading it aloud to Nancy Drew, she gave me a hug and whispered, "the battle is the Lord's."

As I finished my dessert, one thought warred against my mind: was Jonathan still planning on kissing her, or worse yet: had he already?

✱✱✱

"The blood looks so real." I stood across my bedroom mirror, Natalia next to me. A twiggy crown wrapped our heads, and crimson oozed on our faces and splattered our white shirts. We each wore large, cardboard signs. Mine read: *For God so loved the world that He gave His only begotten Son, that whoever believes in Him should not perish but have everlasting life.-John 3:16*

Nati's read: *If you confess with your mouth the Lord Jesus and believe in your heart that God has raised Him from the dead, you will be saved. For with the heart one believes unto righteousness, and with the mouth confession is made unto salvation.- Romans 10:9-10*

My bedroom door opened. Mom, holding a glass of wine and munching on peanuts, halted. "Umm...what are you two doing?"

Natalia slowly faced her, already in somber character. "We're going to Aventura Mall."

"Like that?"

"Yeah," I answered. "We've been praying for the lost and I figured since it's Halloween, we could use it as an opportunity to share the gospel. We don't plan on saying anything, just walking around and letting the Word speak for Himself."

Mom crunched loudly before taking a sip of wine. Dad stepped beside her, a piece of Cuban bread in hand.

"Whoa." Dad swallowed his food and placed his arm around Mom. "What are you two doing?"

Natalia relayed the same information and even divulged on how she used chocolate syrup and red paint to create the blood. Indeed, our faces were supremely sticky, but if it meant someone got to know Jesus, it'd be worth it.

"You both are very creative," Dad said, "I hope it goes well."

"Thanks, Dad," I replied.

"Just be careful." Mom took another sip of wine. "I don't want you ending up on the news in the back of a cop car or something."

Nati walked very slowly out of the room, still in character. "That is definitely possible."

I trailed her. "Blessed are you when they revile and persecute you."

"The godly in Christ Jesus shall suffer persecution."

My heart seared within. Okay, I prayed for Natalia to love Jesus, but I never imagined she'd be as radical as my behind. She'd been so free-spirited when it came to Jesus. Wanna go to this Bible study with me? Yes. Wanna go evangelizing at Hollywood circle with me? Yes. Wanna write this movie script for God with me? Yes. My walking miracle and fellow prayer warrior.

As we walked outside, my phone rang. My Dream Boy.

I cleared my throat and held the phone away from chocolaty face. "Hello?"

"Hey, Natasha, do you have a moment?"

I looked at Nati, carefully placing her cardboard sign in the backseat. "Yeah, what's up?"

"Me and Lily just finished performing our scene in class."

My heart thumped as if I'd just seen the trailer to a super creepy horror flick.

"It came out good. Not that you care."

I definitely do not.

"But I also wanted to tell you that…you were right."

"About what?"

"You were right about kissing a scene partner."

I pressed my still-cardboard-wearing back against Nati's mazda and willed myself not to begin shouting at my boyfriend right before heading out to evangelize.

"I thought I could kiss her just as an actor, but I was wrong. We decided to do a stage kiss, so we never kissed in our rehearsals."

I nearly dropped the phone and broke out in praise, but decided to whisper thanks instead.

"After all the time I spent with her," Jonathan continued in his convicted voice, "I saw how easy it is to start thinking about doing something you didn't intend to do in the first place."

"Yeah, it's called playing with fire for a reason," I said.

"And I almost got burned." Jonathan paused. "The night I almost went to the playground, I felt like I was fighting myself, but you helped protect me."

I climbed into the car. The Lord said it is not good for man to be alone so I will make a helper suitable for him. I love this boy, but he kinda proves God's point. And I know Eve wasn't all that and a bag of chips either. She fell hard, too. Shoot, even David himself, the 'man after God's own heart,' fell in the worst way possible, murder and adultery, but somehow, God was able to use him despite his sin and devastating mistakes. Not without consequence, of course. We do reap what we sow, but repentance does touch the loving Father's heart, who desires to forgive us, seventy times seven. And at the end of each day, my hope is to be more and more like Him.

Natalia bulged her eyes at me as I spoke, breaking character. "The spiritual war for our lives is real. Satan knows our weaknesses, and he will use every opportunity he can to exploit them. If we don't take God serious and are awake to what's happening around us, we'll fall right into the trap."

"Preach!" Natalia yelled as she drove away from our house.

Jonathan and I responded the same: "Amen."

22. New Thing

Where in the blazes is he? I rose from my seat, smoothing out my silky, lavender gown as the lights in the packed sanctuary dimmed. The band made their way onto the gold and purple ornamented stage. I scanned over the flood of people and toward the middle entrance doors. The guitar strummed an upbeat tune as the first song ushered in the beginning of the New Year's celebration. Of all nights, why does he have to be flaky on the one I'm all decked out for? Now he's gonna have to wait until after the worship service when the lights come back on to take in my gown—aka the dress Nati wore for her homecoming. She'd also been missing in action. I was really looking forward to enjoying this special night with both of them.

My gaze travelled to Kelly, on my left in her usual cozy tee and jeans, arms lifted high, and eyes already closed, and then to my right. Dad, in a gray polo, also had his big arms raised. I smiled up at him and rested my cheek on his bicep. He kissed the top of my head, making my stomach warm. I can't complain too much. Kelly could come since she was on Christmas break, and Dad was still an every Sunday and every holiday church-goer. And best of all, he had been growing, slowly but surely. More kind and more prayerful, he'd even took on more opportunities serving the poor, of course.

My smile grew as I remembered that random phone call I'd received one high school morning during the Chris saga, where Dad had been crying because God answered his prayer to feed a homeless person.

Jonathan appeared at the end of an aisle with Natalia trailing behind him. I let out a long sigh as they squeezed through. So he decided to come after all.

"Hi." I kissed Jonathan's cheek as Nati stood on the other side of Dad.

Instead of returning the gesture, he focused on the band. My skin turned cold. What's wrong with him...why is he upset?

I turned toward the stage. Whatever, I'm not gonna worry about it now. I lifted my hands and praised God to the popular Chris Tomlin song.

***

"What's wrong?" I pulled on Jonathan's arm as he and I walked alone in the church's parking lot, slowing him down. The midnight sky seemed as dark as his countenance toward me. "Don't worry about it."

"Jonathan, seriously."

He halted and turned. "What?"

"Can you talk to me?"

He shook his head before striding forward. "It's just that I didn't want to do this, and I go to your house to find you'd already left with your dad."

"But this is what I did last year." I smoothed the silk lavender clinging to my waist, which he still had yet to compliment. "You didn't like it?"

"It was all right, but I wanted to do something else."

I bowed my head as we reached his car. I knew he wasn't sure about coming. He never told me yes or no, and I did remind him somewhat last minute. I should've at least waited for him before leaving. "I'm sorry, Jonathan."

"It's okay," he shut the door with a clank.

"Do you wanna go out, maybe get a bite to eat?"

"No, I think I'm just gonna go home." He opened the driver's side door.

Tears flooded my eyes as I got inside. This isn't how I envisioned celebrating the New Year.

***

Okay something's definitely wrong with him.

The first evening of the new year flaunted itself outside of my bedroom window, watching me and Jonathan as we sat on the floor...

He stared at the laminated "wood," wincing as if terrible thoughts pierced his mind. Whatever mental suffering he's going through became evident soon after he arrived at my house. I'd noticed some anxious chest rubbing the past few days, as if he had heart burn or something, and of course Mom mentioned it—but this...this is next level.

I closed my eyes, a stirring within my soul. God, I don't know what he's battling, but can You please speak through me? Slowly opening my eyes, I set them on my struggling boyfriend. "Jonathan, I know what it's like to feel condemned. But the Bible says, 'Therefore, there is now no condemnation for those who are in Christ.'"

He looked at me, his face full of pain... "But I feel like I'm not going to heaven."

Okay. That's not what I was expecting. I rested a palm on his shoulder, a calm assurance resting over me as the words continued to pour from my mouth. "Well, you can be sure. Why don't you come with me in my backyard and say a prayer out loud, from the heart, asking God to forgive you and for Jesus to come into your life."

"But I already believe in Him."

"I know, but sometimes we believe, but God is still on the outside and God's more personal than that. He wants to be on the inside so He can change your heart."

I prayed silently as he watched the floor again. Please God, let him do this. I know he believes, but Your Word says perfect love casts out fear. Maybe He hasn't given you all of his trust, or He doesn't understand Your Son paid it all, so there's nothing to be afraid of...God's love covers us in Christ, the only perfect child...

Jonathan looked at me. "Okay."

My heart clapped against my chest in excitement as we walked out of my room and descended the stairs. Oh my gosh, this is really happening right now. God You are so good!

Mom washed the dishes as we scuttled past the kitchen. "Where are you guys going?"

"The backyard." I quickened my steps. I don't need Mom to begin a full blown investigation right now.

The moon shone full and bright directly above the concrete slab my parents never used for a shed, as if God aimed a spotlight on the place He knew we'd pray at. As if he was egging us on...

We stepped into the light and bowed to our knees as the night turned still. Not a single breath of air disturbed the peaceful quiet all around us. Even the humidity hid itself.

"Would you like to say a prayer inviting Him in, or let me lead you in one?" I asked.

"You can lead." Jonathan spoke quietly, still so...defeated.

"Okay." I took his hands in mine and began a prayer I'd heard almost every Sunday at my church. After most sermons, the pastor would ask if anyone would like to pray. The words were simple, nothing very poetic or fancy, but yet, they were extremely profound. This humble acknowledgment that yes, we humans are prone to failure, to mistakes, to desiring what we shouldn't at times; the jealousy, the lust, the pride, we've all been there at some point or another, and before a holy God, we're just a broken, helpless mess. Nothing can rectify our past, our present. No matter how good we are, we just can't ever be enough…but Jesus is.

God knew we couldn't save ourselves, we couldn't earn heaven. Jesus came to give us what He alone could receive on His own merit, on His own righteousness. He spoke boldly that He was the Son of God because He is—the only sinless One to walk the earth. And He chose to die in our place, so if we give our heart to Him, if we trust in His goodness rather than in ourselves, we will be saved; saved from God's rightful wrath, saved from eternal separation from Him, saved from our own sin and mistakes, and finally receive the right to become children of God.

I opened my eyes.

A smile stretched on Jonathan's face, a spark in his eyes, his earlier dark countenance now shining with light. "I feel…better."

Salvation for Natalia, and breakthrough with Jonathan. I surveyed the stars. Now this is the best start to a new year I've ever had.

✳✳✳

"And then he said a prayer with you?" Natalia sat across from me at the island, her long waves spilling over her untouched turkey sandwich.

I leaned against the counter and munched on a Cuban cracker. "Yeah."

"Wow..."

"I know. Now eat your sandwich already. I feel bad."

"Oh yes!"

As she finally dug in, my phone rang: My Dream Boy. I quickly swallowed as I answered, putting him on speaker. "Hello?"

"Hey princess, what are you up to?"

"Nothing much, just here with Natalia."

"Tell her I said hi."

Nati leaned over the counter and yelled as if she were on top of Mount Everest. "Hello, brother!"

I smiled as I waved her back.

Jonathan chuckled his husky, sweet, make me wanna kiss 'em chuckle. "I wanted to know if you wanna read the Bible together later?"

I gawped at Natalia. She gestured for me to respond.

"Uh, sure. That'd be great."

"Okay, so I'll be at your house around seven."

"Sounds good, see you then."

"I love you, my Aurora."

"I love you, too."

Natalia brought a fist to her mouth and "choked" on her sandwich as I hung up. "Gross."

"You're the one who introduced us."

"Don't remind me." She smirked. "So he wants to come over to read the Bible. Weren't you praying for that?"

I set my cracker down. "I've been praying that he'd finish the whole New Testament."

She put her sandwich down. "I'm tellin' you girl, when you invite God into your heart, you start to change. It's like suddenly, instead of wanting to hit up the club, you want to hit up church. Instead of smoking a blunt, or getting drunk, you wanna read the Bible."

"Preach it!" I fist-bumped her. God is changing the lives of those I love right before my eyes, answering prayers like wildfire.

Behold, I will do a new thing, now it shall spring forth, shall you not know it? I will even make a road in the wilderness and rivers in the desert. The beasts of the field will honor Me, the jackals and the ostriches, because I give waters in the wilderness and rivers in the desert, to give drink to My people, My chosen.

I smiled as Nati, my newest sister in Christ, finished her sandwich. I guess this is just the beginning.

23. GOOD TO MEET YOU

Jonathan and I bustled through my church's doors and scurried into the main hallway. Being late stinks so ba—I gasped. "Look, it's Pastor John!"

Pastor John, the potential "spiritual father" to our relationship stood a few feet away from the middle doors to the sanctuary, shaking a bald man's hand.

I turned to Jonathan, my nerves going haywire. "Do you wanna meet him?"

Jonathan glanced at the pastor before giving me a tense, "Sure."

I purposed to portray utter calmness as we strode over to our hopefully future spiritual father just as the man he spoke to left. "Hey, Pastor John!"

"Hey, Natasha." Whiter skin hilariously lined his eyes where he clearly wore sunglass for too long in the Florida sun.

I tried not to laugh. "This is my boyfriend, Jonathan."

"Jonathan, my brother, good to meet you." Pastor John gave his hand a brisk shake. "So, when you guys gettin' married?"

My heart nearly lurched into my throat. I stiffened as Jonathan managed a polite smile.

"Well, I know I have to be the spiritual leader, and like the pastor taught last week, I have to carry the weight of leading my wife and children, and I don't think I'm there yet." Jonathan's confession flowed so freely, as if he and Pastor John were sitting in his office having a private counseling session.

"That's definitely true," Pastor John replied, "but that's why you don't do it yourself, God helps you."

Jonathan nodded, and I nodded along with him. Yes, Pastor, preach it! Jonathan doesn't have to be afraid to marry me, God will help him be an amazing husband, I know it.

"All right," Pastor John pat Jonathan's arm. "I'll let you guys get going then. It was great to meet you, brother."

"You, too."

I waved at the kind man who'd so lovingly led me and the other missionaries in Romania, and then followed Jonathan into the sanctuary. That was way too coincidental. Of the four thousand people that attend the Wednesday night service, the one person hanging around our path happens to be the man God wants to be our spiritual father. I may not fully understand why this meeting happened now, but either way, I know Your timing is absolutely impeccable, Lord.

As we hurried into our seats, my pastor took the stage and gave a few quick announcements. "I don't know how many of you in here are young and can act, but our AIDS ministry is doing a show called the Inner Circle for AIDS awareness this fall, and auditions will be Saturday morning, the 27th so if you're interested, there'll be a booth set up in the east corridor with more information."

I squeezed Jonathan's hand. "We have to check that out."

"Totally." He smiled as my pastor continued.

"And we'll be having a beach baptism. That's happening Saturday, April 17th. So, if you've given your life to the Lord and feel like that's a command you're ready to obey, I really encourage you to come out and answer that call. You won't regret it."

I remembered the cool, salt waters of May as he continued the announcements. Last year's baptism was so much more special than the one I did when I was eight in the Catholic Church. This time, I actually knew what it meant, and that it's supposed to be a choice.

As the Pastor asked everyone to join him in prayer before diving into the Word, I closed my eyes and offered a quick prayer of my own. *God, I pray one day Jonathan chooses to get baptized, too.*

24. CHANGE

Powerful. Just Powerful. I shut off the lamp on my night table, and crawled into bed, last Wednesday's message once again coming to mind. Jonathan and I chose to go to the young adult service, where a man in his twenties shared his testimony. God brought him from a swimmer who lost his scholarship over a drunken party that caused someone to die from alcohol poisoning, to a man willing to die for a friend when threatened by a gang member while evangelizing in Brazil. Russ's story not only left a mark on my heart, but on Jonathan's as well.

After service, Jonathan approached one of the young adult leaders, some blue-eyed surfer named John, and signed up to the guy's men's Bible study! Yet another thing I've been praying for Jonathan that got answered right before my flipping eyeballs!

To think, all of these prayers being answered one right after another, it's almost like God's...preparing Jonathan for something...

Ring.

I snatched my phone off of my headrest. My Dream Boy. I smiled as I answered. "Hey, handsome. How was the men's Bible study?"

"It was awesome!" Usually calm, cool, and collected Jonathan, spoke as if he'd just gotten out of a gym. "That guy John is intense. All of those guys are so in love with God. There's four Johns in the group, including me."

I matched his enthusiasm. "God is hilarious. I'm so glad you made some godly friends."

"Me, too. Oh, and babe, we really have to practice our purity. After talking to those guys, I don't even want to kiss you until our wedding day."

My heart leapt. Say what now? Wedding day? Is Mr. Not Gonna Get Married Until I'm 26 finally thinking about holy matrimony? No—don't jump to conclusions. He's just encouraged by his new friends who obviously don't believe in sex before marriage either. "That's fine with me."

"Oh, and I'm not hugging girls anymore when I say hi. I'm just going to shake their hand."

Ember's snake-like eyes materialized in my mind like a monster emerging from an ominous fog. Lord, forgive me. I shirked the vision from my mind. "I'm really fine with that."

"Natasha…" Jonathan put on his resolute voice, but this time, a new passion backed it. "I wanna get to know your heart. I wanna love you for who you are, not for how you make me feel."

I sighed into the phone.

"And not just that, but I wanna respect you and protect your name. And I don't wanna sleep over anymore because even though I'm on the couch, I don't want your neighbors to think anything otherwise of you."

Still lightheaded, at least the muscles in my mouth remembered how to speak. "I agree."

"I wanna court you and prepare your heart for marriage, for the man who's blessed enough to have you as a wife."

I sat up, the lightheadedness vanishing. "What do you mean? I want that man to be you."

"I want it to be me, too, but it's something you really have to pray about to see if it's what God wants because marriage is a huge commitment."

I slumped onto my mattress again. As much as I hate to say it, he does have a point. And if God doesn't want us to get married, I should trust Him. I've already messed up too many times by trusting my feelings and my foolish, run-ahead-with-your-emotions heart. "You're right, but I really hope it's you…"

Jonathan spoke with a twinge of sadness, almost as if preparing for that not to be the case. "I do, too."

***

"So how'd your audition go for that AID's ministry show?" Dad—shirtless as always—sprawled out on the Florida room couch as Jonathan and I sat on the loveseat.

"It went really well." I ruffled Jonathan's beautiful, black, shampoo model hair. "The director had us do the Pledge of Allegiance as if we were opening for a rock concert—and Jonathan ran around the room with his shirt off."

As Dad cackled, Jonathan shrugged. "An actor's gotta do what he has to for the part."

I cracked up, too when he came out of the audition room with his hair messy and a big ol' Chuck E. Cheese smile on his face. I only heard him yelling, but wish I could've seen the act firsthand. Actually, seeing Jonathan without a shirt on probably isn't a good thing if I'm trying to keep my thoughts toward him pure.

My phone vibrated in my pocket. An unfamiliar Broward area-code number. "Hello?"

"Hi, Natasha?" A familiar sounding man said.

"Yes."

"This is Tom, the director of the Inner Circle."

I jolted to my feet and mouthed the words 'It's Tom' to Jonathan. His eyebrows shot up as he gestured me to keep talking.

"Oh, hi, Tom."

"How are you doing today?"

"I'm wonderful, you?"

"I'm doing great, thank you. Well, I was calling because I would love for you to play the part of Kat."

I twirled around in a circle and danced for a few seconds before answering. "I'd love to!"

"That's great to hear! I'll be sending out an email with the rehearsal schedule soon. You really embody Kat, and I think we have an awesome cast. Well, I still have to touch base with the others so we'll speak again soon."

After I gave a professional farewell, I screamed.

Dad put the remote down. "You got a part?"

"Yes! I'm Kat!"

"Why am I not surprised." As Jonathan hugged me, his phone rang.

I pulled away. Oh my gosh. Could that be—

"Hello?" A smile grew on his beautiful mouth. "Yeah, that's awesome. Okay. Definitely. Thank you. You, too." He hung up, his smile widening. "I got cast."

I squealed and flung my arms around him.

Dad chuckled. "Would you look at that. You both got in. Congratulations."

"Thanks, Dad!" I turned to Jonathan. "What part did you get?"

"Mark."

"Oh…" What I gathered from the script, Kat was dating another character…

"I wanna thank God," Jonathan said.

"Yes, of course!" I followed him into the living room, excitement permeating my heart. He's really been…flourishing. I seriously never imagined Jonathan could get any more beautiful than he already was, but

I suppose until we die, we're all like living works of art, ever changing, becoming more complex and beautiful as time goes on.

Jonathan held my hands as we stood before Mom's leather loveseat and then bowed his head. "Father, thank You for blessing me and Natasha with this opportunity to be in a show we know will bring about good. I pray that it brings you glory. Thank you so much. In Jesus' name, amen."

"Amen." I smiled at my dream prince. What are the chances that out of everyone who auditioned—and there only being four parts—that Jonathan and me both get in? This is just awesome. I'm so glad we're gonna get to work together. I can't wait!

25. REBIRTH

I can't believe this is happening.

Guitar strings and poetic lyrics that praised God filled the air as Jonathan and I walked onto the warm sand, Bibles in tote. The sun sparkled in his eyes as we passed the "Baptisms" sign, his white shirt brightening his countenance all the more. This all feels surreal, like in moments I'm going to wake up in bed and find that this whole thing was an elaborate dream. It was only three months ago Jonathan said that prayer with me in my backyard, and already he's read the entire New Testament. I was literally there when he finished, and now I'm about to witness his baptism. So many prayers are being answered it's making my brain spin.

Now to Him who is able to do exceedingly abundantly above all that we ask or think, according to the power that works in us...

"Jon, my man." A bronze-skinned twenty-something guy with a lip ring and also in swim shorts like Jonathan approached us.

"What's up, brother?" Jonathan said and they embraced. He turned to me after releasing him. "JD, this is my girlfriend, Natasha."

"Oh, it's nice to finally meet you." JD shook my hand. "We've all heard some really good things about you."

Jonathan shined so hard. "JD is one of the brothers who go to John's Bible study."

"I'm second John," JD said.

I smiled. "Nice to meet you, second John. I assume you're getting baptized, too?"

"Yes, ma'am. I'm super excited. I gave my life to God six months ago, and He's just radically changed it. He saved me. I mean literally."

"Daddy!" A little brunette, maybe three-years-old, ran up to JD, a shaggy-haired, blue-eyed guy beside her.

"This is Melissa, my daughter," JD said as she clung to his leg. "Say hi, Melissa."

I smiled at her. "Hi, princess."

She smiled back and then hid behind her dad.

"What's up, third Jon?" The shaggy-haired guy hugged Jonathan.

"Jason, this is Natasha, my girlfriend."

"Ooh." Jason broke out into a beam as he shook my hand. "So this is the girl you told us about. It's a pleasure to meet you. Jon has said some great things about you."

"So I've heard." I looked at my boyfriend, sun-kissed life-guard complexion a bit pink on the cheeks. Maybe now he understands how I feel the majority of the time I'm with him.

The guitar strumming ended.

"I think that's our cue to go over there," Jason said.

"Right." Jonathan led the way to a crowd seated before a large speaker and microphone stand.

A man in a baseball cap carrying a Bible stepped in front of the mic and bowed his head. "Heavenly Father, we're gathered here today to proclaim publicly our dedication to You. God, I pray with this bold step, that these here would be drawn closer to You. May You bless them as they commit this simple act of obedience, in Jesus' name, amen."

I grabbed hold of Jonathan's hand as the base-ball cap guy introduced himself as Pastor Jim, and asked everyone to open their Bibles to Romans. As he expounded on how baptism represents how Christ died and rose again, and it's symbolic of us also dying to our old life and living a new one in Him, I gazed at Jonathan. It's true, my old life is so far gone. It feels like ages ago that I was drinking away the pain of vicious relationship cycles, being down more than up; desperately searching for love in all the wrong places, as they say. Now I have Jonathan, whose old life is also being buried right before my eyes.

Pastor Jim closed his Bible. "There will be several deacons in the water and volunteers guiding you at the shore. God bless you all for coming out here this morning."

"Well." Jason looked at the water. "You guys ready?"

"Yeah." Jonathan smiled as we all rose to our feet. "Let's go."

I held his hand as we sauntered to the glittering ocean's edge. I can't believe he isn't nervous. Not that I was nervous, but my dad wasn't a strong Catholic who believed I was joining a cult. Will his parents ever forgive him for leaving behind what he'd been raised in for nineteen years…?

A volunteer in an orange t-shirt waved us over. "Are you all getting baptized?"

"No." JD gestured to himself and Jonathan. "Just us two."

"Okay. Do you guys wanna go together?"

"I don't mind." He looked at Jonathan.

"Yeah, bro. Let's go."

My eyes watered as they walked into the sea toward two older men. The waves pounded, and the men laughed at their force. I did as well. Resolute Jonathan, standing in the midst of intense waters, ready to leave it all behind, and face the threatening storm ahead.

His family liked me, but they didn't exactly like the idea of Jonathan going to a new church. To them, the focus wasn't Jonathan growing in His love for God, growing in passion and knowledge of the Word; experiencing deep friendship with those who felt the same burning desires as he did; the desires to stop living in their old ways, and embrace the new life hidden in Christ. Jonathan wasn't abandoning God, He was simply walking closer to Him and experiencing Him like his parents still had yet to. But maybe some day they'd understand.

Jonathan faced away from the waves as the men and JD waited for them to calm. A minute passed and finally, a moment of stillness. The sun reflected off the water around him, making him glow like an angel. The guys held him as he leaned back and allowed the waves to rush over him. He rose from the deep, a smile of victory on his face.

26. CONFIRMATION

"Lord, I also pray for my sister to keep growing in You and putting You first. I pray that Marilyn comes to know You. I pray Jonathan keeps growing and becomes the spiritual leader You've called him to be, and Lord, bless us in marriage. In Jesus' name. Amen." I slipped off my bed. I don't know why I've been praying that last part for the past three days. I mean, I've wanted to marry Jonathan since before week two, but I haven't actually prayed for it to happen anytime soon…

"Natasha, Jonathan's here!" Mom yelled from downstairs.

I trotted out of my room and into the hallway. My heart thumped softer as Jonathan peered up at me behind his thick lashes. His gorgeous smile fueled mine.

I scurried down the steps and hugged Mom goodbye.

"Okay, have fun at your youth service! I love you."

"I love you, too."

"Bye, Mrs. Sanchez," Jonathan said as she followed us outside into the clear evening.

"Text me when you get there!"

I shook my head. Perhaps one day I'll understand what it's like to be a mom.

"After you." Jonathan held open the passenger door for me. Heat still managed to warm my face at this kid's chivalry. He turned on the car and a man sang to a catchy tune. "This is the song I told you makes me think of you."

"God gave me you for the ups and downs," the man sang. "God gave me you for the days of doubt. For when I think I've lost my way, there are no words here left to say, it's true, God gave me you."

"Aww, Jonathan—"

"Especially this part..." The man continued, saying how it'd been a divine conspiracy that such a lovely angel would fall for him.

Tears moistened my eyes. "I love it."

"It's exactly how I feel." He gazed at me with his dreamy hazel eyes before driving away from my house. Gosh, how could I not fall for him? He said I blow every girl he's been with out of the water. Well, he really blows every guy I've been with out the universe.

"So…" Jonathan put on coerced casualty. "What would your dad think if we got married at a young age?"

I pressed my shoulders back into the seat. Wait, wait, wait. Did I really just hear that?

Jonathan glanced at me.

"Um, he wouldn't care," I said a bit quickly.

"He wouldn't?"

I tried to make my shoulders relax. "Well, he's always been one to stay out of my relationships. After I unknowingly brought a twenty-six-year-old over when I was eighteen, he said, 'I trust you. As long as you're happy and he doesn't physically hurt you.'"

"Wow. If I have a daughter, I'll be the opposite."

"My dad's always trusted me. I had a lot more freedom than my sister in high school because I didn't get into much trouble. He'd be happy if I was happy. And you're very different than the guys I'd bring home. Very."

His mouth turned up. "Where would you wanna live?"

"I don't mind. An apartment I guess." My adrenaline kicked in, speeding up my heart rate. Why is he asking me these questions? I can't believe he's asking me these questions! "I mean, eventually I'd like to live in a home where there's mountains around and there's four seasons, but it takes time to get up to that point so in the beginning I don't mind where."

"I don't mind either. But I think it's good to stay close to our families, at least when we're starting out."

"I agree."

My mind sprinted into action. Is he considering—No. You've let your heart run ahead of you too many times before and had it crushed in the process. Maybe he listened to a sermon on the radio about marriage or something and just had it on his mind.

I looked out the window at the starlit sky, pushing thoughts of marriage to the very back of my mind. Your will be done, Father, not mine.

***

There he is again! In the same place he stood last time!

Toting my Bible, I grinned at Jonathan as Pastor John walked through the dispersing Wednesday service crowd. Simple polo on, he approached. A smile stretched across his sun-burned face. "So guys, when are you getting married?"

Jonathan gave his hand a very serious, manly sort of shake. "Why don't I take your number down so we can meet."

I held back a squeal as I squeezed my Bible. He's actually getting Pastor John's number? It feels like forever ago when I went to Romania and prayed that prayer about a spiritual father and had that convo with Pastor John about it. But maybe Jonathan's just preparing for the far future…a far future that included marrying me someday…?

Pastor John got his number and asked, "When are you free?"

"Wednesdays, Thursdays—"

"Thursday sounds great. How about next Thursday the 29th we meet here at the cafeteria around four?"

"Yeah, four sounds good."

"Great man, I look forward to it. Well, I gotta go guys, enjoy the service. Keep growin'!"

"Thank you." He shook Pastor John's hand again before he walked down the hall.

I cuffed my arm around Jonathan's and strolled into the sanctuary. Could this really be happening? We're only twenty-years-old! I remember how after things failed with Chris, I figured I'd never get married. But then I fell in love with God, and was so content in His perfect love, and met Jonathan out of nowhere, the boy of my dreams—literally. And now, a little over a year later, here I am, with Mr. Blow 'Em Out of the Water making preparations to marry me?

We slipped into a row as the band began singing, 'How great is our God.'

Well, no matter what happens, God, You are so great and amazing, and You will always be more than enough for me.

I know.

***

Should I ask him, or just leave it alone?

I glimpsed at Jonathan as we stopped at a red light just a few blocks away from His House Children's Home. The afternoon sun arrayed him in light, his purple button down reminding me of the way it had shined on him the first day we met as we drove to my church. Why would God sculpt such a beautiful piece of art? He can be so distracting at times.

The stoplight turned green. Dang it. I don't have that much time to think this through. Ah, whatever.

"So, what did you and Pastor John talk about?"

"More like, 'What did Pastor John talk about?'" He chuckled. "I barely got a word in, but it was great."

I held back a laugh. Yes, the man was a pastor for a reason. He did love to yap, but his words were always helpful and fun. "What did he say?"

"Well, he was talking about purity and how when the pastor says, 'You may now kiss this bride,' he says the 'now' for a reason. So I really wanna try even harder to not kiss you until—God willing—we get married someday."

I pouted. We haven't been doing perfect on our kissing fast, but I don't mind that we slip up sometimes. "But what if that's years from now?"

"Well, think of how amazing and so much more meaningful it's going to be. It'll also make me appreciate being able to touch you more. And it'll strengthen my love for you because since we're not touching, I get to love you for your heart, not your body or the way you make me feel. It makes me less selfish because I'm not gaining anything, I'm just getting to know your heart better."

My heart thumped slowly. "I wanna marry you so bad."

Jonathan reached over and took my hand. "We should pray about it. Ask God to confirm if He wants You to marry me, and I'll do the same."

We pulled up to His House. Ask God to confirm if He wants me to marry Jonathan? Why didn't I think of this before?

"I will," I said as I opened the passenger door. "Thank you for dropping me off."

"No problem."

"See you later."

"See you, princess."

I scuttled out of the car and up to the doorstep of house twenty-three. I looked over my shoulder before walking inside. Still arrayed in light, Jonathan flashed one of his perfect smiles at me and then drove off. Gosh, I can't wait to pray about God confirming if He wants us to get married or not.

"Hi, Miss Natasha." Ms. Lisa appeared in the hallway, sweat dripping down the sides of her round face, a sign of the children's recent arrival from school.

"Hi, Ms. Lisa." I gave her a quick hug. "I'll be right back, I'm going to the restroom."

"Of course."

I scampered into the large blue bathroom and got into one of the stalls.

"Dear Lord, please show me if You want me to marry Jonathan or not. Give me confirmation. In Jesus' name. Amen."

As soon as I walked out, sweet Shaundra wrapped her skinny little arms around my waist. "Miss Natasha!"

"Hi, Shaundra. Did you follow me in here?"

She beamed while nodding.

"You crazy girl. Come on."

She held my hand as we traversed into the living room and then raced over to adorable, honey-haired Monique, seated on the floor playing with dolls.

"Hey, kids." I waved at the Haitian children gathered around the dining table playing memory with a deck of cards. They waved back, smiling before they continued their game. They're so joyful. You'd never think that they just came here from a devastating earthquake and that the majority of them are now orphans. Thank God for places like His House.

Ms. Lisa rattled a toy to a baby girl in a carrier at the corner of the room.

I rushed over to her. A cast covered the infant's caramel colored hand. "Oh my gosh! Is this the Miracle baby, Jenny?"

"Yes, ma'am," Ms. Lisa said. "She was only two months old when they found her stuck under the rubble for four days with nothing to drink."

My heart ached for the precious little doll in pink. "May I?"

"Sure."

I carefully took her into my arms, her soft skin like silk. "Hi, Jenny."

She smiled at me, her light brown eyes agleam with love.

"She's beautiful. And she looks great!"

"She sure is. She still has to wear this cast, but this hand's fine."

Jenny squeezed my index finger with her good hand.

"I can see that." I laughed as I carried her to an armchair, Ms. Lisa beginning to mop around the table. I can't take my eyes off of this baby. "God has big plans for you, huh Jenny?"

She giggled as Lavinia trotted up to me.

The ends of her purple-beaded braids jingled against one another as she thrust a card in my hand. "For you."

"Why thank you." I smiled as the other miracle child trotted back to the dining table. I remember when Ms. Lisa told me Lavinia's legs were crushed so she needed a walker. The doctors said she'd never be able to walk again without it. But then on Easter morning she was suddenly able to. It's so incredible how unlimited my God is.

I looked at the card Lavinia gave me. No way. I blinked a few times as if the picture on it would morph into something different. Okay, this is just insane. A boy with long brownish-black hair and green eyes stood beside a life buoy, the title 'Life guard' underneath him.

I peered up at Lavinia, playing jubilantly with the other children at the table. With the huge pile of cards scattered across it, what are the chances she gives me one of a life guard that even looks like Jonathan? It's not like she's ever met him or knows my boyfriend's a life guard. Was that a confirmation?

"Hello." A brunette, older than me, stepped into the living room.

"Hello, Ms. Marie," Ms. Lisa said as she continued mopping.

I took a picture of the card with my cell before forcibly putting it down. "Hi, Marie, I'm Natasha. Are you a volunteer?"

"Yes I am." She strolled over to the armchair and shook me and Jenny's hand.

"How long have you been volunteering here?" I said.

"I just started a week ago actually. I'm originally from Connecticut, but I moved here recently with my husband."

Connecticut? Where Jonathan was born?

I tried to contain my hysteria. "That's great. Welcome."

"Thank you." She walked over to the table and greeted the other kids as I smiled at Jenny, a barrage of joyous, fluttery feelings overloading my heart.

"I can't wait till you grow up and get to know God. He is so awesome."

27. THE SIT-DOWN

"That is pretty weird." Jonathan gazed at me as I sat down in a stool beside him at Mom's kitchen island. The golden light never fails to make him look like he walked straight out of a dream from the fifties. He shook his head before continuing. "It's funny…when I was at John's house for Bible study, he had told me about his confirmation for Kate, and after that I really wanted one for you." His smile brightened up the room as it always does. "The guys ended up surprising me for my birthday. As a joke, they gave me this gift bag that has the Disney princesses on it, and it has two flaps that open where the picture of the door is, and Sleeping Beauty and Cinderella were standing inside it."

"Wow."

"I know. They didn't even know that I call you my Aurora and Cinderella."

"That's so random." I laughed. It's too random, actually. Too random to be coincidence. My laughter ceased. Maybe God does want us to get married…

"Hey…" Jonathan set his elbows on the counter, forcibly casual. "Can you maybe go and visit Marilyn, or do something for an hour or so?"

I arched an eyebrow. "Why?"

"I wanna talk to your dad about something."

I sealed my mouth shut to keep it from gaping. Talk to my dad about something? Oh my gosh! Could he be…Okay, control yourself, Natasha. Just breathe and remain calm. "Um, okay, that's fine." I slipped off of the stool and skipped to a kitchen drawer to get Dad's car key. "See you in an hour." I pecked his cheek before walking outside into the warm and lovely afternoon.

Everything grew brighter as I cantered to the car. Would Jonathan really ask Dad for my hand? I mean, what else could they talk about that requires me to be elsewhere? Oh Lord, if he really is asking my dad if he can marry me, please let him say yes! I don't think Dad's going to be super thrilled—me and Jonathan aren't exactly rich and we're only twenty-years-young—but I don't think he'd say no…at least, I hope not.

✳✳✳

An hour never dragged so long in my life. I gripped Dad's sun-faded steering wheel, ignoring how uncomfortable the bruised leather felt against my choke-hold. I mean, Dad loves me, he would want what'll make me happy. He'd say that about the no-goods I used to bring home, so why would he withhold Jonathan from me, as wonderful as he treats me and as much as I love him? But then again, these guys weren't asking for my hand in marriage. If that is what Jonathan was asking…

I pulled into my driveway as the brightness of the sun dimmed behind a chunk of clouds. My front door opened and Jonathan walked onto the porch, accompanied by towering Dad, actually in a shirt for once. They shook hands all professional like, and then Dad walked back inside. I hopped out of the car as Jonathan approached.

"Hey." I studied Jonathan's face.

Forehead smooth, mouth relaxed, he played placidity oh so well. "You wanna start heading out? There's probably gonna be traffic."

"Uh sure. Let me just return my dad's keys." I trotted inside, my stomach suddenly queasy. No smile from Jonathan, not even a smirk. That's not a good sign.

Dad stood by the island, chomping on a banana as I dropped his keys in the drawer. "Hey, Tash."

I froze. "Hey, Dad."

He set the banana down carefully like if it were a handgun and walked over to me. I held my stomach. Oh no, I don't think I'm ready to hear what he has to say.

He wrapped his big hairy arms around me and gave me a gentle squeeze. I hugged him back. Oh gosh, is this an, 'I'm sorry' hug? But why would he say no? Me and Jonathan both believe we received confirmation. But we can't get married without my dad's consent, can we?

Dad released me. "I love you, Mama."

"I love you, too Dad." I hastened back outside before I could burst into tears.

Jonathan stood in the same spot—still quite placid appearing. I lowered my head as I followed him to his car. I guess our confirmations were just coincidences.

My queasiness subsided as we sat in the car, hollow sadness now replacing it. I suppose there'll never be a good time to find out why Dad said no.

"So, what did you and my dad talk about?"

Jonathan focused on the road. "Don't worry about it."

The sorrow surged up to my heart, tears piling up in my eyes as I peered outside.

"But would you like to go to that place you told me about on 163rd street? The one you went to with Marilyn and Alice a couple of months before we met?"

I turned to him, my gloominess dissolving. The jewelry store? The place where I looked at engagement rings, and Marilyn said, 'Natasha, you're not even engaged, let's go,'—embarrassing me in front of the Asian saleswoman? I tried to tone it down a knotch, but failed. "I'd love to!"

Jonathan smiled as I removed my cell from my pocket. So Dad said yes after all! Okay, okay. It's 5:15. Service starts at 6:30. I gazed out at the bumper to bumper traffic as we crept along Ives Dairy Road. All right, Lord, if this is really Your will, let me find a ring in five minutes. Engagement ring hunting is super exciting—heck, it's nothing short of amazing—but not missing service is more important to me. You, God, are more important to me.

Twenty minutes dragged by as Jonathan's car crawled off the expressway, escaping the back-up on 95. I checked the time as we parked at the 163rd Street mall. 5:35. In order to make it to church on time we have to leave by 5:40. I bustled out of the car and raced inside. Despite my terrible memory, we miraculously made it to the store with four minutes to spare. Jonathan held my hand as we approached the ring counter.

"Hello." The same pretty and slender Asian lady that helped me when I came with Alice and Marilyn walked over. "How may I help you?"

"I came here almost a year and a half ago to look at engagement rings when I was single," I said, "and my friend embarrassed me."

She chuckled. "Oh yes, I remember you."

"Well, I'm here again and I'm with someone now." I couldn't refrain a grin as I turned to my dream prince.

"I see." The woman smiled as she gracefully led us to a glass counter with an array of gold and silver rings. "These are our engagement rings."

I glanced at Jonathan. He tightened his grip on my hand as a small smile turned his mouth up. I quickly peered over the glass before I could start crying. Too big. Too much. Too square. Hmm. A white-gold ring with a flower-shaped diamond glimmered near the bottom of the case.

"That one's pretty," Jonathan said.

"Which one?"

He pointed at the flower-shaped one I had my sight on.

"I was just thinking the same thing!"

The saleswoman unlocked the cabinet and removed the pretty ring. She fit it onto my finger.

"It looks perfect on you," Jonathan said.

I bat my eyes as I wiggled my fingers, the ring gleaming as it caught the light. It's so me: dainty and feminine. And it's not too much, but just right.

"This one was originally nine hundred, but everything is half off so it's four-fifty," the woman said.

"Only four hundred and fifty dollars?" I reluctantly took it off and handed it back to her.

"And you can put in on lay-away and pay the rest later."

I looked at Jonathan.

The bright lights in the store shined off his magnetizing irises. "Are you sure you like it?"

All I could do was nod.

"You don't wanna look around at other stores?"

"I guess we can." I glimpsed at the competing jewelry store across the way.

"We'll be back." I jogged over to it, Jonathan following beside me.

"Hello, welcome." Another Asian woman stood behind the jewelry counter. "What can I help you with?"

"Engagement rings please." She gestured to the glass case in front of her.

I scanned over the diamond rings, most of them bulky and square, and way too diva-like. "Thank you." I faced Jonathan.

"You like the other one?"

"Yeah."

"Okay." He thanked the woman for her help and then held my hand again as we walked out. A gleam of sadness dimmed his luminous eyes. "I don't have the money yet."

"It's okay." I looked back at the jewelry store that detained my ring. I just hope by the time he does it's still there.

I smiled at him as we traversed into the parking lot. Either way, the ring isn't what matters. I don't even care if the engagement ring I rock is a fifty dollar one, just as long as I have one, I'm happy. Apart from the amazing beauty of knowing my Savior, His great love for me, and having assurance of eternal paradise with Him, Jonathan is one of the greatest gifts I could ever receive. What's more important: the size of the ring, or the man giving it?

Jonathan kissed my forehead before opening the passenger door for me. I dipped into the chair like melted chocolate. Thank You so much, God. Because of Your grace, the man I'll someday receive a ring from is one who knows and loves You. What more can I ask for?

28. FIRST CLASS

When God is moving, things move around to accommodate His will—even our own plans.

I looked around at the three dozen couples seated across the risen platform in the church's banquet hall. And then my sights settled onto Jonathan. Sitting beside me with his super dark hair and piercing eyes, his soul now even more beautiful than his appearance. It was months ago—after the first meeting with Pastor John failed—that I went to our church's information desk and asked for a sign-up packet for their seven week premarital classes. I never showed Jonathan that I had them. I knew he wasn't ready. But then time goes by and he starts changing...growing. First, it's just a few marriage questions in a car ride one night, and then, next thing you know, I'm picking out my engagement ring.

These premarital classes were right around the corner, but Jonathan and I had rehearsals for the Inner Circle on the same nights of the classes. Then literally out of nowhere, Tom tells us the show is cancelled —the week before premarital classes begin. And now here I am, sitting at a table with Jonathan in a room with forty people who hope to build a solid foundation before they say, "I do."

I smiled at my dream boy as a stout, middle-aged man carrying a Bible walked onto the risen platform and stood before a microphone.

"Hello everyone, I'm Pastor Dan, the premarital pastor here. I know you all are excited to embark on this journey to marriage, but before we get started, I just wanted to share a verse with you. It's Isaiah 43:19–20."

My gaze locked onto Jonathan. Did this pastor really just say the verses God gave me for Jonathan when I asked if he was the one? That night in my room, when I cried out to God and flung open my Bible, not understanding how Isaiah 43:19-21 related to my question, so God told me to read it in the Amplified, which made it very, very clear. In fact, if it weren't for those verses, I might have ended things with Jonathan.

Pastor Dan opened his Bible. "Behold, I will do a new thing, now it shall spring forth, shall you not know it? I will even make a road in the wilderness and rivers in the desert. The beasts of the field will honor Me, the jackals and the ostriches, because I give waters in the wilderness and rivers in the desert, to give drink to My people, My chosen."

My heart galloped in my chest like a wild race horse as Pastor Dan closed the prophetic book.

"I read this to you because sometimes, marriage can be really refreshing, overflowing with water, but there are also times where it can be dry and rough. But God promises that for His people, He will always make a way in the wilderness and send rivers in the desert. Will you pray with me?"

I held Jonathan's hand as I bowed my head. I can't believe he just read those verses. That has to be yet another confirmation, right?

Pastor Dan prayed a sweet prayer over the group of romantic hopefuls, and then smiled as he opened his eyes. "I'm going to ask Butch and Karen to come up and share their story with you."

A balding yet handsome man accompanied by a tall brunette with a wide smile walked onto the platform.

Butch took the mic and said, "I'm actually gonna let my wife, Karen share our story." He handed over the microphone and her big smile suddenly faded.

"Well, before Butch and I got married, we were living together with my twelve-year-old son." She glimpsed at him and he gave her an affirming nod. "We had both recently become Christians and were engaged, and wanted to get married here. In our first class, the counselors strongly suggested moving out if any couples were living together."

Her husband kept his gaze on her as she bravely recounted their story.

"I made excuses like how I really couldn't afford to live on my own, especially with my son. So Butch and I would sleep in separate rooms, but that wasn't working very well because we'd tiptoe down the hall and sneak into each other's room at night."

I watched Jonathan from my peripherals. Although his attention appeared to be on Karen, he probably did the same undercover observing with me. We'd fallen prey to the trap of too much proximity and privacy. It's called, flee "youthful lusts" for a reason, but instead, we were making room for it— literally.

She blushed and giggled before turning serious again. "I knew what we were doing wasn't right in the Lord's sight so I gave God an ultimatum. I said, 'Lord, if You really don't want us living together, make a way for one of us to leave.'"

Now Butch laughed, garnering a sideways glance from his bride.

"The next day our neighbor, who happens to be a Christian, knocks on the door and says, 'I was praying and just felt that I needed to tell you that I turned my garage into a room and you can stay there, free of charge, if you need to.' At first I was like, 'Great, why can't he be the one that has to leave,' but I am so thankful that it was me because being stuck in that garage with no TV and nothing to distract me made me get into the Word and I just got to know God better." Eyes agleam, Karen's wide smile returned. "I grew so much that year. It was like God wasn't only building our relationship, but also preparing me for marriage." She left the microphone, and taking her hand, Butch led her back to their seats.

I wiped my eyes as Dan took the stage again. "The wedding is just one day and then marriage is for the rest of your lives. It's a very serious commitment, and you want to make sure you're on the same page. The Lord uses marriage not to make you happy, but to make you holy. Not that there aren't amazing moments, but two sinners sharing life together"—the majority of the room laughed—"it can and will get rough. Especially if one of you is a Christian and the other isn't."

I peered at Jonathan as the laughing quickly died down. Thank God we're both Christians and on the same page now with our beliefs. I know people who think what they believe doesn't affect their relationship, but it's different when you're serious about your faith because it shapes how you view every aspect of life. I can't imagine starting a family with Jonathan if we weren't in agreement on how to raise them.

As Dan offered another word of counsel, Jonathan kissed my hand, right where the purity ring still adorned my finger—and hopefully, where a real wedding band would someday replace it.

29. SPECIAL OCCASION

"Just wear a bathing suit under," Jonathan called from downstairs.

I pranced around my room as I tried to squeeze into a pair of shorts. "But why?"

"Because, it's the Miami Seaquarium. You'll probably get wet."

"Fine." I yanked my shorts off and slipped into a bathing suit before squirming back into them. I hate wearing shorts, hence the reason my six-year-old pair doesn't fit me anymore.

"Come on, Cinderella, we have to go," called again.

"Okay, I'm coming." I threw my shirt on and scurried into the hallway. I halted as I saw him. His hair had been shaved on the sides and now choppy on the top, revealing even more of his clean-shaven face. Gosh he's gorgeous.

Jonathan smiled as I descended the steps. "We kind of have to hurry." He strode outside into the hot, almost-summer afternoon.

I jogged to keep up with him. Goodness, I don't know why he's in such a hurry. It's only twelve o'clock. I'm sure the Seaquarium closes at five the earliest.

Jonathan threw open the passenger door for me and then dashed into the driver's seat. "I take 95 South right?"

"Yes."

"Okay."

I surveyed him as he sped toward the highway. This is very unlike him. He's never in a rush, even when we're late for something. I guess the show or whatever it is starts at a certain time and if we don't get there we'll miss it.

We arrived at the Seaquarium in less than twenty minutes and without getting pulled over. As soon as we parked, Jonathan got out and trotted toward the blue building. He paid for our tickets and hovered over the map he'd received like Ethan Hunt's character in Mission Impossible. "This way." Stuffing the map in his pocket, he sprinted up the steps past a sign reading, *Paradise Cove*. Behind the building, dolphins swam across a huge pool.

"Oh my gosh!" I pointed at them. "Look, love!"

Jonathan smiled as he held open one of the doors to a gift store. "Come on."

I scurried inside and ran across the store to the other end where a pair of glass doors showcased the pool of dolphins. Tears filled my eyes as the shiny gray creatures glided across the water more smoothly than a cruise ship. Young women in white t-shirts motioned to the lovely sea animals and they turned over onto their backs. I chuckled as a pretty blonde rubbed one of their bellies. I've never seen dolphins this close before. Last time I came here, I was too young to even remember them.

"All swimmers follow me this way please." A tan young guy in a wetsuit strolled over and opened the doors as Jonathan and a few others followed behind him.

"Wait," I said. "Are we swimming with the dolphins?"

Jonathan grinned at me as the wetsuit guy and the others traversed outside.

"Oh my gosh!" I jumped up and down a few times before embracing him. "Jonathan, this is incredible!" I pulled away and gave him a light push. "So that's why you were in such a rush."

He held the door open for me. "I wanted to surprise you."

I gaped at him as we walked over to a counter where the other swimmers gathered, collecting wetsuits. I giggled as Jonathan handed me one. I seriously can't believe this is happening right now. "How much did this cost?"

"A lot," Jonathan said as he grabbed a suit.

"Yeah...I don't think I wanna know actually." I hurried into the bathroom to change. How this kid topped horseback riding on the beach, I'll never know.

I slipped into the unflattering suit and then skipped outside and froze. Wow. Jonathan beamed as he stood in the sunlight, the blue and black highlighting those ethereal eyes and perfect skin. He looks like a freaking superhero. Okay, okay, Natasha, don't lust. Think about the dolphins.

"All right, you can go into orientation over there"—Wetsuit guy pointed to a room across the bathrooms—"to get a quick training before you go on Dolphin Odyssey."

I snatched Jonathan's hand and veered into the small room. Let's get this over with so I can swim with my new favorite creatures already. I tapped my foot as the brunette intern explained how to engage the dolphins. After ten minutes she finally shut off the projector. "And last of all...have fun!"

I jumped up faster than the nine-year-old girl on the other side of Jonathan. He laughed as he followed me outside.

The pretty blonde I saw playing with the dolphins earlier waited by the door. "Hey guys! I'm Lauren, one of the dolphin trainers here at Miami Seaquarium. You can follow me right this way."

"I'm so excited," I said as a brunette trainer led the rest of the group to the opposite end of the pool.

Jonathan's eyes gleamed as we followed Lauren inside the water. He's such a sweetheart. How many guys think of taking their girlfriends swimming with dolphins, or horseback riding on the beach? Jonathan really acts like a dream prince. I thank God that He made him such a romantic. Romance is something every girl appreciates —me especially. And oddly, I appreciate even more now that it's coming after our friendship and the spiritual. It feels like finally being right side up, after having been comfortable upside down for so long.

An hour flew by as Jonathan and I played with Ripley, our designated dolphin. It's amazing how intelligent these creatures are—mimicking the way sharks swim, allowing us to kiss them, gliding across the water on their tailfins! I must say, out of all the recreational activities I've done in my life thus far, this one totally takes the cake. And what makes it even more special is that my future husband is the one who took me here.

Lauren gestured for me and Jonathan to turn around. "If you guys can just turn this way and pose for a picture. Ripley's going to jump out of the water behind you."

Jonathan twined his fingers in mine, water splashing behind us as the photographer snapped a photo.

"Nice job, Ripley." Lauren tossed him a fish. "Okay, now you're going to get to ride Ripley across the pool. He's going to swim by you, and just clasp your hands around his fin and he'll take you across."

"Oh my gosh, that's awesome," I said as Lauren signaled Ripley. He swam by me and I grabbed hold of his fin. He surged forward. The salty water hit my face, stinging my eyes as we cut through to the other side. I spit out the gross water as I released him and landed on the platform, a photographer taking photos of my not-so-successful finish. I just had to ride a dolphin like a drunken mermaid. How embarrassing.

Ripley had already swum back to the other side. I rubbed my eyes as Jonathan latched onto him. Unlike me, he strode gracefully above the water, his Colgate grin making him look like the poster boy for dolphin riding, or the hot young merman on a book cover. Well, at least one of our photos will come out nice. I smiled as he released Ripley and floated beside me.

"That was awesome," Jonathan said.

"It was, but I think I did it wrong because I practically drowned on the way over here."

His grin disappeared. "Are you okay?"

"Yeah, I'm fine." I cupped his cheek. One day I'm going to marry this gorgeous and caring young man. Hopefully…

A dolphin swam over to me, a large white container in its mouth.

"What's this?" The brunette trainer said. "Looks like Echo has a gift for you."

"Aw, thanks, Echo." I removed the container. There must be some sort of dolphin souvenir in here. Gosh, how awesome is this? I've got a giant sea creature delivering goods like I'm the Little Mermaid, —the ungraceful version. I twisted the container open. My body stilled and my heart missed a beat.

The engagement ring I chose rested on a piece of red velvet.

I faced Jonathan, tears already forming in my eyes.

His smile faded as his hazel eyes made everything else disappear. "Natasha, may I have the honor of cherishing you as my wife?"

I slapped my hand over my chest and whimpered, "Yes."

Jonathan stepped closer and took my hands. This really just happened. Jonathan Sapienza, the man of my dreams, the guy I would have hoped for all of my life had I known he actually existed, just asked me to be his wife. Is he perfect? No. Am I perfect? Definitely not. But this I know, we're perfect for each other.

The photographer took pictures as Jonathan led me out of the pool. We only took a few steps before he dropped to his knee.

"Natasha Danelle Sanchez, will you marry me?"

I nodded, every inch of me blazing with joy as he shakily slid the ring onto my middle finger. "Wrong finger, love."

"Oh."

I giggled as he put it on my ring finger. I looked around at the small gathering. I guess I would be nervous too if I were him—and pledging to be a husband six years sooner than planned.

"Give her a little kiss!" The photographer egged.

Jonathan kissed my hand before rising to his feet, and then fixed his gaze onto mine. "Just for the special occasion?"

I squeaked out a, "I think it's fine."

A smile grew on his mouth, and then he slowly leaned in, for a sweet, brief kiss as the camera clicked one last time.

30. DISRUPTION

My grandma's living room quickly turned into a war zone.

She leaned over in her armchair, her tone now venomous and her beady eyes trailing me as I sat beside Mom on the couch across from her. "You guys should just wait for two years so your mother can throw you a nice big wedding with a nice reception. But you're all rushy rushy."

"We don't care to have a big wedding, Mama." I glanced at Mom, mouth twisted in a frown, her gaze avoiding mine.

My throat became drier. "And I appreciate that my mom wants to give us a nice reception, but we don't care too much for that either. Being married is most important to us. Saying our vows before our closest family and loved ones and before God is all we care about."

My grandma seemed to slice me to pieces with her stare. "You know, just because you dream of getting married doesn't mean it's going to happen. Not everyone's dreams come true. You're probably going to get pregnant and then what?" She sucked her teeth. "You're setting yourself up big time and you're too blind to see it."

I stood. "Okay, Mama, thank you. You're right. I have to go now." I kissed her cheek and strode outside. The late afternoon sun beamed mercilessly on the little fifty-five-year-old-and-plus parking lot. I understand her concern, but marrying Jonathan is something I believe God approves of—something I believe He planned and has been blessing all this time. But Mama had been around much longer than me. She got married at sixteen, three years shy of my age. They eventually got a divorce. Maybe she was right...

I yanked my cell out of my pocket as I flung open the passenger door of Mom's civic. Plopping into the seat, I texted Jonathan.

Maybe we are rushing things. Maybe this isn't what God wants. Let's just not get married.

Tears ran down my face as Mom got into the car. She moved a strand of hair behind my ear. "It's okay, Mamashmoo, you know how Mama can be. She can be hard, but she loves you. Don't worry, we'll have a nice reception, I already spoke to Dad and took some money out—"

"No, Mom. I already told Jonathan we shouldn't get married."

"Oh, Mamatu, you didn't have to do that." Her eyes watered. "You're going to get married and we're going to get your wedding dress today."

My phone chimed. My Dream Boy.

Okay, Natasha.

I tossed my cell into the cup holder and began to sob. "He s-said o-okay."

"He's hurt, that's all. You just told him you guys shouldn't get married very unexpectedly."

I sniffled. That make sense…Gosh, I'm such an idiot! Now not only am I hurt, but I just hurt the man I love, too. I called him.

"Your call has been forwarded"—I hung up. Great, he doesn't even wanna speak to me now! Oh Lord, what have I done?

I tried again. "Your call has"—I put the phone down and bowed my head, my body quaking from my sobs. "Please God, c-calm me d-down. I'm so sorry I let my emotions get the best of me again. Please touch Jonathan's heart and work this out for Your good."

Oxygen flowed freely to my lungs, dispersing itself through my body, carrying with it the peace of my Heavenly Father. My breathing evened, the quakes slowed, and hope reignited. "Thank You. In Jesus' name. Amen." I texted my fiancé.

I'm so sorry, Jonathan. I was at my grandma's and she said just because I dream of being married doesn't mean it's going to happen, and I started crying and just acted on my emotions. I love you so much. We're going to get my dress now, and on September 10th, I'm going to walk down an aisle in white to you.

I looked up at Mom. Tears still fell from her tired eyes. I quickly mopped my face and then embraced her. "It's okay, Mamatu. I apologized to Jonathan. Hopefully he understands."

She nodded as I released. God, please let him understand. I don't know what I'd do if he decides not to marry me. I don't know how many flipping times I've punched this kid in the chest with a stupid emotionally-led decision. It's coming down to the wire. Our wedding day is fast approaching. If I were him, I'd second guess marrying the Queen of Unpredictable as well.

Chime.

I hesitated before opening the text. Your will be done, Father.

I love you too, Natasha. You can't let people's opinions get the best of you. That's what they think, but we already know what God thinks, and that's all that matters.

Relief surged into my heart. Thank You, Lord! So much! And Jonathan's right. The wedding is a month-and-a-half away. The enemy is going to do everything he can to prevent two Christians who love Jesus from meeting at the altar. Come to think of it, he's been trying to break us up since the very beginning. It kind of excites me actually, because it must mean that God's gonna do great things through our union…

I smiled at Mom. "Let's go look for that dress."

31. HUNTING

Apartment hunting isn't as fun as I thought it'd be.

Marilyn's mom stopped at a red light in the quaint, Aventura golf-course neighborhood. Bright lights shined on the small green hills that seemed to ripple ahead endlessly. This will be the seventh apartment Jonathan and I visit in person, not to mention the twenty or so we saw online, and so far nothing's worked out. Our wedding— I smiled despite our situation—is less than three weeks away. Finding a place is a must right now, or else it's the guest room at his mom's house.

Carol pulled in front of an apartment building, off-white like her platinum hair. "We're here."

I forced a smile as Jonathan and I followed her outside. Poor thing offers to be our real-estate agent with no idea it would turn out to be Mission Impossible.

Jonathan held my hand as we stepped into a squeaky elevator. I mean, I don't wanna stress him out before our wedding.

We've been so happy and relaxed, just filled with aw and excitement that God wants us to be husband and wife. We've been attending premarital every Wednesday night, reading Love & Respect together, and paid off all of our debt in two-and-a-half months. I even left Honey's and got a higher paying job at Houston's. But the fact that we still don't have a place is a little frightening.

We walked out of the elevator and trailed Carol down an outdoor hallway. She stopped in front of a door numbered 706. "Here it is."

The door opened as she dug through her red Louis Vuitton. A tall woman in a pink dress-suit stood in the doorway. "Carol?"

"Yes, hello."

"Hi, I'm Lavern, the owner."

"It's good to meet you." Carol shook her hand. "And this is Jonathan and Natasha."

"It's good to meet the adorable couple." She smiled as she stepped inside. "Well, come on in." She led us into a charming, sandy-colored living room.

"I love the colors," I said.

"Oh, there's a view." Carol strolled over to a pair of sliding glass doors and we followed her onto the balcony.

Lavern pointed at a strip of water. "There's the bay for the boats, and right over there is the Water Ways."

"I used to go there a lot for a time." I squeezed Jonathan's hand. "It's really nice. They have good restaurants and a light tower with a lake view. It's super romantic."

He nodded, evidently not impressed. My shoulders drooped as Lavern led us through the rest of the apartment. Oh, Lord, please let him like this place. I really wanna be alone with him when we're married. I don't wanna have to live with someone else—especially not parents.

After a quick tour of the 1,000 square foot apartment, we followed Lavern back to the living room. Elegant yet humble somehow, she turned to us. "So, what do you think?"

"I love it." I glimpsed at Poker-Faced-Mime Jonathan. "I mean, I have to see what he decides. We're getting married in a few weeks."

"Of course. Where are you getting married?"

"At a nondenominational church in Fort Lauderdale."

"Oh, so you guys are also Christians?"

"Yes, we are." My grip tightened around Jonathan's. I'd say it's nice that our potential landlord is a professing Christian.

Carol removed a paper from her bag. "I know you're asking for 1,050, but they were looking for something less."

"I mean, it's a little negotiable," Lavern said. "What were they looking to pay?"

"Nine-fifty."

I held my breath as Lavern contemplated the offer. Please let her be okay with it, Lord. Out of all the places we've seen, I really like this one.

Lavern gave us a genuinely warm smile. "Nine-fifty is fine."

"Fantastic!" Carol said a bit too emphatically. "So, do you want it?"

"We'll think about it," Jonathan replied. "There are still some places we haven't looked at."

She raised a perfectly waxed eyebrow before facing Lavern. "Okay, I guess we'll be in touch then."

"All right. It was nice meeting you all." She walked us to the door.

"It was nice meeting you, too." I shook her hand. "God bless you."

She smiled that sincerely kind smile at me again. "And you as well."

I trudged back to the elevator, my faith —and my patience—surely being tested. It is such a cute place, and for this area the price isn't bad. And I'm pretty sure Lavern's a good woman, and to have an understanding and caring landlord is a huge blessing. The wedding's dawning quickly; we really need a place.

We reached Carol's Cadillac, and Jonathan held the passenger door open for me. I avoided his eyes as I got inside. Please Lord, if it be Your will, let him say yes to this place.

Just wait.

I looked at Jonathan through the rearview as he stared up at the black sky.

Okay, Father. I trust You.

***

My cell vibrated as Jonathan and I sat down in a middle row in the sanctuary.

"Hello?" I whispered.

"Hi, Natasha, it's Carol."

"Oh hey, Carol what's going on?"

"I spoke to Lavern and apparently there's another couple that wants the apartment so I need to know if you and Jonathan have decided yet."

I glanced at Jonathan as he read our church's newsletter. Another couple? Dang it. He hasn't so much as said a word to me on the topic. "Um, I'm at church right now. I'm going to speak to him, and I'll call you back."

"Okay…"

"Okay bye." I dropped my phone in my purse just as the band walked onto the stage. "Um, Jonathan…"

He lowered the leaflet. "Yes?"

"I really liked that apartment…"

"You did?"

"Yeah. I really, really did."

A smile curled the ends of his lips. "If we move there, will you be a happy princess?"

As I nodded, his smile widened.

"Then it's yours."

"Oh my gosh! Yay!" I threw my arms around him and held him tightly. I can't believe he said yes! Now all I have to do is talk to Carol, and if everything works out, we'll have our first place!

I kissed his cheek as the band started their first song. So no living back home with the 'rents after all. Thank You, Jesus!

32. UNITY

Okay, I know they're older and they just want what's best for us, but are parents always right?

Even though the open kitchen and living area stretched spaciously and had high ceilings, the air around Jonathan's mom's dining table became stuffier and stuffier by the millisecond. Seated beside me, Jonathan slipped his palm into mine as his mom served mine and Natalia.

With perfect auburn hair and a tidy button-blouse, Jonathan's mom was the older, female version of him. "My concern is that it may be a little too much for you guys right now," Julie said as she set two plates down for me and Jonathan. "And Jonathan's lifeguard job is going to be over in the middle of October and he still hasn't found another job."

I glanced at Natalia before answering. Her look read, 'Be careful.' "I understand and appreciate that you only want what's best for us, but I know my God will provide.

Luke chapter twelve says, 'Don't worry about what you're going to eat or drink, or what you're going to wear, for your Heavenly Father knows you need these things, but seek His kingdom first and everything else will be added to you.' I believe in that promise. And I know you are moms"—I looked at Mamatu as Julie sat beside her—"but Jonathan and I have Jesus. He'll take care of us."

They exchanged looks before Julie answered, a sincere glimmer in her Jonathan-like eyes. "That's beautiful, hon'."

"I mean, Mom," Jonathan said, "Carol called us after she spoke to Lavern and said the other couple that was looking at the apartment left Lavern a voicemail saying they wanted to rent it and she heard Carol's message right after that and she decided to call Carol back first. Do you think that was a coincidence?"

"I know, Jonathan, but you can just get a cheaper place and save up for a year and then get a nicer one."

"I'm going to get another job, and we can afford it now."

Natalia gestured to a pink-frosted cake on the kitchen island. "So Julie, what kind of cake is that?"

I gazed at Jonathan as Nati, mom, and Julie chatted about dessert. I don't want my future mom-in-law to be so worried about us. It makes me feel terrible. And I know they really want a reception...

"Maybe we can just do the wedding next year," I whispered to him, although putting off the wedding is the last thing I wanna do.

"No. We're getting married September 10th. We already pushed it up a month for them. I wanna be your husband. I want you to be my wife."

I couldn't help, but smile. It's true, we can't please everyone, and like Pastor John said when we met with him, we have to start marriage by making a stand together now if we're planning on becoming one later. His words entered my thoughts as Jonathan peered into my eyes...

For most people, when they're first starting out, it's tough. When I got offered to be a pastor, I took three times less than what I made in my other job. But I was able to provide for my family better with less, living pay check to pay check, than when I had more. Now I'm comfortable, but man, honestly, I miss the days when I was forced to depend on God because it was the closest I've ever been to Him and it brought me so much closer to my wife. Don't worry so much about the wedding, guys. My wife and I

didn't even have a wedding, but we've been married
for thirteen years, and every day is a honeymoon.

33. THE UNFORESEEN

"Dace called me. He's coming over to talk." Marilyn's words delivered a chill through my spine as I sat at the bench behind Houston's, the sun setting over the lake where a plane once crashed.

"But why?" I spoke into my phone. "You haven't seen, or even spoken to each other in over a year, and the last time you did it was about me."

"Exactly. Why else would he need to talk to me?"

"But I don't get it. I thought he hated me. What would he need to talk about?"

"I don't know. Maybe he knows you're getting married in two weeks and needs some closure."

"That makes sense. But how would he know I'm getting married?"

"Uh, maybe his sister," Marilyn said.

"Oh, that's right. Jonathan had movement with her last semester and they had a scene together, and when I went to his school once, I saw her and told her about the engagement."

"Well, there you go."

"But it's been a year since I've seen Dace and the last time we sort of communicated with one another it wasn't a very happy exchange. And I'm pretty sure he's still with August. Shouldn't he be over it by now?"

"I guess we'll find out."

I looked at the time on my phone: 5:57. "I have to get back to work. I'll call you when I get out."

"Are you going to tell Jonathan?"

My stomach twisted. "I'm not sure. I don't want him to get insecure…he doesn't really like Dace for obvious reasons, but I don't know yet."

"Okay, but make sure you decide soon, Tash. This is important."

"I know." I looked at the dark sky as I hung up, my churning stomach worse. The last time I saw Dace in person, he said if I ever needed him, he'd be there for me. But then a couple of months later, he texts me, and when I told him to listen to a song with apologetic lyrics for all the times I've hurt him in the past, he sent one back that basically said, 'Go screw yourself.' It was as if Aridon had finally won the fight, and Dace was lost forever.

I walked up the ramp toward the restaurant's entrance. Well, whatever his reasoning for reaching out to Marilyn, the timing of all this is too impeccable. I think I know who inspired Dace to do this, and his motives for doing so aren't good.

***

I walked out of Houston's, my legs tired from the long day of hosting. As I slipped out of my blazer, the October evening chill breathed on my skin. I headed to the same bench from earlier, when Marilyn called with the news. The cold air would've bothered me, but tonight, it soothed my aching body and awakened my weary mind. As ready as could be, I called Marilyn.

"I'm out."

"He just left," she said. "Expect a phone call."

I gazed ahead at the black lake. Great, now I have to tell Jonathan. "What did he say?"

"Well, he definitely doesn't hate you."

"That's a relief. It kinda sucked feeling like someone I cared about hated my guts."

"He actually said he felt bad for the way he's treated you. Oh, and he wanted to see you."

"Yeah, that definitely wouldn't have been good."

"He was insistent on calling Jonathan to ask him if he could. I was like, 'Dace, trust me, you should not call Jonathan, and I am not giving you his number.'"

I laughed. "Thanks, Mar. Jonathan's grown a lot, but I don't know how well he would've taken that."

"I know. And, Tash…he said he still loved you."

Say what? "How is that even possible? I haven't seen him in a year and we don't talk anymore."

"Well, he said he wasn't in love with you, but I know he was lying."

"How do you know?"

"I asked him if there was no Jonathan or August, would he be with you, and he said that question was irrelevant and that it doesn't matter what he wants because you're about to get married in two weeks."

"Wow." I closed my eyes on the ebony waters and prayed. Lord, please let what happened to me happen to him one day. That he falls in love with You, and his heart is completely mended. In Jesus' name, amen.

"So…" Mar said slowly, her cautious Bestie-Mom tone in full play, "are you going to tell Jonathan?"

"Yeah, but after Dace and I talk." I don't know how Jonathan's going to react. I mean, it's not like I'm going to see Dace or anything. But would Jonathan call off the wedding for this?

Beep.

I looked at my phone. The number rang a bell. "I gotta go, he's calling."

"All right, Tash. I love you."

"I love you, too." I stared at the number on the white screen before answering. Here we go. "Hello?"

"Hi." Dace's tone sounded serious, but something seemed different…

I watched the swaying waters. "How are you?"

"I'm all right," he said. "So I assume you spoke to Marilyn?"

"Yeah. She told me some of what you spoke about…about feeling bad for the way you've treated me."

"Yeah." He exhaled into the phone. "I know I haven't been…the kindest person to you, and I wanted to apologize for that."

"It's okay, I know I've done a lot to you, too, and I apologize for that as well. But thank you, I really appreciate it."

"I really would have preferred seeing you in person, but Marilyn convinced me otherwise."

"Yeah...I'm not too sure how August would have reacted, but I know Jonathan wouldn't have liked that very much."

Dace chuckled. "Yeah, I figured as much, but I thought I'd give it a try anyway. And surprisingly, August was very understanding. She's even okay with us being friends."

Whoa. Red flag. "Um...Jonathan wouldn't like that either and I understand. I mean, we were very intimate with each other at one point. It's kind of inappropriate."

He spoke lower. "I guess that makes sense."

Beep.

I checked my phone. My Dream Boy. Oh gosh. "Uh, can you hang on for a sec?"

"Yeah."

I clicked over, my hand suddenly shaky. "Hey, love."

"Hi, beautiful. Are you home yet?"

"No, my dad should be here soon, but can I call you back?"

"Okay. I love you."

Guilt trickled into my heart. Poor thing doesn't even know that I'm on the other line with his nemesis. Gosh I hope he takes it well when I tell him. "I love you, too, Jonathan." I hesitated before clicking back over. "Hello?"

"I'm here."

I gazed up at the moon, ready to end this conversation. But before I do, there's one thing I need to know first. "So how's your relationship with God?"

"That"—he sounded as though he spoke with a smile—"well, running my own gym didn't work out so I'm stuck in this less than minimum wage job, making four twenty-five an hour, cooking food in a restaurant. I think He's really trying to humble me."

I laughed. Pride is definitely something Dace struggled with. "Humility is a character trait He honors a lot."

"Yeah. And I'm still going to church on Sundays. August comes most of the time."

"Church attendance is good, Dace, but God is very personal. He desires us to spend some alone time with Him, too, and more than just once a week. Reading His Word, listening to Him, allowing Him to teach you, is very important."

"Yeah. I definitely need to start reading again. Maybe then He'll see I'm trying to do good."

"Remember when you told me you didn't think you wanted heaven?" I said.

"Yes…"

"Do you still feel that way?"

He sighed. "No, I don't. But honestly, I'm not sure if I'm good enough yet to get there."

"Don't forget what Christianity is about. No one's perfect. The Bible even says in Psalms, 'There's no one that does good, no not one.' No one is 'good enough' for heaven. If we were, Jesus died in vain. But we're not, hence God putting on flesh and coming to earth to live out the perfect life we couldn't so that in His willing sacrifice, the price for every sin could be paid once for all. We only have to put our faith in that, turn away from our sin, and run to Jesus instead, then we'll get heaven. For 'It is by grace alone that you have been saved, not by works, lest any man should boast.' Remember that, Dace."

"Thanks, Natasha." His voice lowered again like before. "Well, I guess this is goodbye. I'm sorry again for everything."

My eyes began to water as a small weight lifted from my shoulders and a sense of peace replaced it. "I am, too, Dace. Thank you for all the times you were there for me."

"I've said it before and I'll say it again, I'll always do my best to be there for you, even if this is the last time we speak to each other."

"I appreciate it."

"Well, if I don't see you again in this life, hopefully I'll see you in heaven."

I smiled as a shooting star raced across the sky. "You will, Dace. You will."

***

Okay, I'm in trouble. Big trouble.

"Why didn't you tell me earlier?"

I lowered the volume on my phone and hugged my pillow as if doing so would protect me from Jonathan's extremely convicting disappointment. "I didn't want your mind to be racing and worrying while me and him were talking so I thought it'd be better to tell you after it was done so I could tell you everything that happened at one time."

"But the fact that you weren't sure if you were going to tell me bothers me. It's like you have something to hide."

"I didn't want you to get insecure. That was my mistake." My eyes watered as the fear of losing Jonathan skulked into my heart and began choking it. "In the future, I won't hesitate to tell you things anymore. I have nothing to hide. I love you, Jonathan." I held my breath so I wouldn't sob into the phone. Please, God, our wedding is less than two weeks away. If something happens with Jonathan and me, I know I'll eventually get over it, but I don't wanna have to. I wanna marry him. I want him to be my husband.

Jonathan's silence propelled my fears, my hopes of marrying my only dream prince now on the verge of being tossed into the fire. Pieces of my heart seemed to pull away from the center, ready to break off and fall like ashes. If he calls it off, I will experience the heart-break of a lifetime, worse than those that came before it, and be sentenced to yet another healing surgery from my Heavenly Father that would likely take much longer than six days to complete.

Jonathan breathed into the phone. "I love you, Natasha Sanchez."

I swallowed my sobs and laughed with joy instead. "Soon I'll be Mrs. Natasha Sapienza."

34. THE EVER AFTER

I always wanted to have a story like Cinderella and Princess Aurora's, one that had the magic of Cinderella's and the romance and adventure of Aurora's, with a prince as handsome and brave as Philip. Someone who would sweep me off my feet in our first meeting, a man I could only dream about—and did—like Aurora had. A prince who wouldn't be afraid of riding through a path of thorns to get to me, who would conquer dragons—the devil himself—to take me in his arms and carry me to the altar. Well, now I'm living an even greater fairytale—a real life one.

"So you and Jonathan really don't want to go to a hotel room?" Marilyn said as she parked us in front of my new apartment building. "Natalia and I have the money, the offer still stands."

"We've already decided being alone together in our first apartment is more special than a nice hotel room. He's in there decorating our bedroom right now." My heart danced in my chest at the reminder.

"Oh, there's Jonathan!"

I ducked. "What is he doing? We're not supposed to see each other!"

"I know." Marilyn grinned as she stepped out of the car. "He's just helping me carry up the lamp so you guys can see what you're doing tonight."

I squinted at her as she disappeared to the back of her new, baby-blue Hundai. The trunk opened and then closed after a moment. I counted to thirty before taking a peek.

Jonathan carried the black standing lamp into the building, Marilyn trailing him. Gosh, even the back of his head is gorgeous. I eased deeper into the passenger. I can't believe I'm marrying him. Two years ago I would've never imagined there was truly a man out there that was perfect for me. I opened the text message he sent earlier.

Today you're going to become Mrs. Sapienza. Today we're going to become one. I love you, Natasha, and can't wait to tell you, 'I do'.

I closed my eyes. This all feels almost surreal, like it's too good to be true, but I guess that's what it's like when God's the One who's writing your love story. I wish I had known Jesus like I do now years ago. I wouldn't have wasted all that time on guys who weren't the one, and gone through all the drama and heart-break I suffered. But, I'm grateful that at least now I do know Him, and I never have to go through another heart-breaking relationship again. Oh my gosh.

I opened my eyes as I sat up. Where's Marilyn? It feels like it's been at least ten minutes. We have to arrive at the church and get our hair done. Aimee's been waiting!

I called Mar.

"Hello?" She sounded as though a grin stretched her mouth.

"Marilyn, why are you taking so long? We have to go to the church. Aimee's waiting, no one's showed up yet."

"Sorry, I got…distracted. I'm coming down now."

I furrowed my brow as I hung up. Distracted? For ten whole minutes? Oh, I know why she got distracted. She obviously got a sneak peek into what Jonathan's doing to the bedroom.

Adrenaline quickened my heart rate. I'm kind of frightened, but at the same time, I can't wait…

Marilyn reentered the car. "Sorry about that." She slowly shook her head. "Wait until you see it. He wasn't even done and it was beautiful."

I beamed as she pulled out.

"And I don't want to know how much he spent on it all."

My smile vanished. Oh gosh, I don't either. I'm all about economizing, especially now that we're both out of debt and taking on the responsibility of marriage. But whatever, it's for the second most special night of my life. And there isn't really a price tag for what I plan on giving him tonight, but the fact that he spent a lot to make it special for me does show how much he values it.

I looked at the time on my phone, my already fast-beating heart pumping faster. It's 1:30. Only four more hours and I'll be walking down the aisle to the man of my dreams.

***

The seven-by-seven foot Bridal room quickly turned toasty with all the female bodies packed inside it like perfumed sardines.

"Aimee, her hair looks beautiful!" Mom, decked in indigo, covered her mouth as Mama, Natalia, my also-indigo-clad bridesmaids, Alice, Isabelle, Marilyn, and Mimi, ooh'd and ahh'd in agreement.

My stout, Cuban hair stylist trimmed the long bang falling alongside my cheek and then held a mirror up behind me. An intricate weaving knit my hair half-up and half-down, the ends of my bright, blonde tresses falling in soft curls.

"Wow, Aimee," I said. "Thank you."

Mom lifted my chin. "Oh and your makeup, Mamashmoo, you did such a good job! You can be a professional!"

I touched my cheek as Natalia and a few of the others girls agreed again in many yes's and amen's. I hope Jonathan feels the same.

Two knocks pounded the door.

Aimee lowered the mirror. "Who is it?"

"Faith!" The Souther and super-pregnant, wedding coordinator bustled into the room, her white-blonde hair tousled as if she'd been chasing chickens around. "The groom finally got here, but it's already six ya'll. Are you almost finished?"

"Yes, yes." Aimee shooed me off the chair.

"Let's get her dress on!" Marilyn said.

Dark-haired and gorgeous Mimi surveyed me with watery, turquoise eyes. "You look like Barbie, mi hohia," she said in our trademark, just-off-the-boat Cuban accent.

I laughed as she jumped onto a chair and helped Mar grab my twenty pound dress off the rack. "Thanks, girl."

"Mom, where's her underskirt?" Natalia's question caused everyone in the room to freeze.

"Oh no," Mom said. "Don't tell me I left it!"

"Mom! The skirt was essential so the dress isn't dragging under my feet!" I pursed my lips. Okay, just relax, Natasha. It's a wedding, something always goes wrong.

"Maybe Dad can go get it."

Faith leaned back, her prego-belly bulging threateningly. "He doesn't have time, momma."

"Crap. I can't believe I did that!"

"Does she really need it?" Marilyn tugged on my veil-like skirt. "This dress is pretty poofy as it is. It looks like it already has an underskirt."

I eyed her. "I do, Mar."

"Wait!" Faith said. "We might have a donated one. What size are you?"

"Four." I plopped into a chair as she scurried out of the room. "Please, Jesus, let her find one."

Mom trudged beside me. "I'm sorry, Mamashmoo."

"It's okay."

Marilyn held her cell. "It's 6:15, Tash."

Mimi hopped off the stool. "The groom can wait!"

I brought my knees to my chest and hugged them. Jonathan, my groom, is somewhere in the vicinity. I wonder how he's doing. Is he freaking out, or is he at peace? I mean, despite this whole underskirt dilemma, I'm not anxious at all, probably because I prayed about this day and asked God to help me remain calm and not cry. I know if I start crying, I won't stop for a while, not to mention my makeup would be ruined.

The door flung open. Faith barged inside with an underskirt. "I got one! It says size eight, but it looks small so try it anyway."

Mom snatched the skirt from her hand and helped me slip into it. "It fits perfectly!"

My anxiety disintegrated as she, Mar, and Natalia fluffed it. "Thank You, Jesus!"

Alice zipped the back as Mom and the others stood.

Mar gaped. "Oh my gosh, Natasha, you're gorgeous."

I grinned as all the women in the room did their agreement fawning. I remember when I showed Mar the bridal magazine that featured my dress without telling her which one it was, and she specifically said mine was ugly. I must admit, the photo definitely didn't do it justice.

Mama clapped her hands. "The veil!"

Aimee grabbed it off the counter and pinned it to the top of my head.

Faith opened the door. "Okay, ladies, I need all of you to get in your places for the ceremonial procession."

"I love you, Mamashmoo!" Mom kissed my cheek before scurrying into the hallway.

Nati hugged me with that gentle, sweet, hug, full of Christ's love. "I love you, sister. You're stunning."

"Thanks, sister." I stared at myself in the mirror as Mama and my bridesmaids followed her out, leaving me alone with my thoughts. The sequence on my strapless bustier and the trimming along my veil glittered in the florescent light, while my skirt fluffed out like the dress Cinderella wore to the ball. I've never seen a more beautiful dress—it's better than I could've ever imagined.

The music for the Bridal party procession started. I beamed as I grabbed my skirt and swayed to the romantic orchestra. You're moments away from becoming Jonathan's wife. From this day forth, he will always be yours, and you will always be his.

The door cracked open. My young, brunette florist carried my purple and white orchard bouquet. "You can come out now."

I breathed in as I took the bouquet and walked out of the Bridal room. Faith stood by the two open wooden doors of the chapel, Dad waiting close by in a classic, black tux. A smile lit up his face as I approached. "You look beautiful, Mama." He kissed my cheek as I placed my arm in his.

I can't imagine what's going on in his heart. This is the walk every father dreads. He's giving his little girl away into the protection and provision of another man. That really says a lot about what he thinks of Jonathan. Jonathan...I smiled, my heart beat hastening at the thought of my fiancé, who stood waiting for me at the altar at this very moment.

A slow and dramatic violin cued our entry, Faith gesturing us to start walking. Dad followed my slow pace as I inched forward, the music growing louder with each step. Satin bows adorned the oakwood pews where my friends and family rose as I entered. Purple petals and ivory candles lined the aisle that led to the altar.

My eyes found Jonathan's, standing beside Pastor John. A lighted cross shined behind him, making him glow. His crisp black tux matched his hair, and he wore the most brilliant smile I've seen on him to date.

As Dad and I reached the end of the aisle, Pastor John read from a small paper he carried. "Who gives this woman to be married to this man?"

"I do." Dad lifted my veil and kissed my cheek before taking a seat.

Jonathan took my hand and led me to the altar as Pastor John addressed the gatherers.

"I don't have any question as a pastor that it's God that brought this couple together today. What you see here aren't two people that were lonely and looking around the world that ended up running into each other. These are two people that God ordained to put together."

Jonathan's grip tightened, his green eyes smoldering with love.

"You guys don't know this," Pastor John proceeded, "but a little over a year ago, I led a mission trip to Romania and that's where I met Natasha. And Natasha began to talk about this young man, Jonathan. 'Pastor John, there's this guy, Jonathan, and I really like him.'"

Our friends and family laughed at his impersonation of me.

"And I said, 'Well, just continue to pray and be patient and let God do it.' And we came back, and over time, all of a sudden I began to run into them. And I got to see who this Jonathan was that she had talked about on the trip. And it was really a special time because I got the opportunity to spend time with Jonathan"—He turned to him—"and hear what God is doing in your heart and your love not only for Him, but for her."

Jonathan's smiled faded as a deep intensity abided in his gaze. I mouthed the words, 'I love you.' He mouthed them back as Pastor John continued.

"Well on that trip in Romania, when I mentioned this thing called courtship, Natasha listened very intently because that's what she desired. She didn't desire to have a worldly dating relationship. She desired something real and intimate and personal, and she wanted it to be with one man—forever."

Jonathan's eyes welled with tears. I almost feel bad now for praying that I wouldn't cry.

"What was really precious to me is that I asked Jonathan and Natasha to write down the story of what God had done. This morning in my office, as I prepared for this wedding and read over their letters, it was crystal clear that the Lord is the One that put them together. They even shared similar things, and I know they didn't talk about it."

A hint of warmth coated my cheeks as I remembered asking Jonathan this morning to read me what he wrote. He totally denied me, saying he wanted to save it for tonight at the apartment...I forced my focus back on Pastor John's speech.

"But what really blessed my heart was seeing their obedience to God and working through this covenant called marriage. You see, they didn't just show up here. They went through a series of premarital classes. They have really sought counsel to make sure they do this right. Besides that, both of you have a real relationship with your Lord and Savior, Jesus Christ."

I nodded, beaming at the name of the first love of my life, who blessed me with a second.

"You both have the support of your family and friends that sit here today, but I know sometimes the road traveled to get here had some bumps, but you got here. Which leads me to the question, why? With three hundred and ten million people in the United States, it always blows my mind how the Lord can create these two people and you end up together. So I asked this question: 'Natasha, there are a lot of great men, why this man?' And this is what Natasha said, 'He's humble, he's my best friend. He makes me laugh, he is my knight in shining armor, he is my dream prince. He gives me support and encouragement, he is sweet and thoughtful. He is tender and delicate toward me, and he is godly. I love him.'" He flipped the paper over. "And then I asked Jonathan, 'There are a lot of women out there, but you chose Natasha. What was it that made you want this woman specifically?' And here were the things that he said. 'Look at her, she's the most beautiful girl in the world. She's my earth angel. She's my fairytale—my princess made real—my Cinderella.'"

I laughed at Jonathan's sweet and poetic words. I can never get enough of him calling me his Cinderella.

"'She's committed and loyal, she is noble. She is so encouraging and generous. She is a woman who seeks after God's heart. I love her.'"

I sighed, causing Jonathan to beam all the brighter as Pastor John opened his Bible. I really can't wait to kiss this dreamy man again.

"Genesis 2:18 says, 'The Lord God said it is not good for man to be alone. I will make a companion who will help him.' You guys are entering into a sacred covenant." He continued to read from Ephesians five about wives submitting to their husbands, and husbands loving your wives just as Christ loved the church and gave Himself for her.

Pastor John closed his Bible and turned to Jonathan. "I've been married long enough to tell you, if you love your wife as Christ loved the church, Natasha will never have a problem submitting to you. But it starts with you, Jonathan, being that man that really loves and serves faithfully his wife. But what is love? First Corinthians says, 'Love suffers long and is kind. Love does not envy, love does not parade itself—it is not puffed up. It does not behave rudely, it does not seek its own. It's not provoked. It thinks no evil, does not rejoice in iniquity, but rejoices in the truth. It bears all things, believes all things, hopes all things, endures all things. Love never fails.'

"Now here's what's beautiful—if God is love and love never fails, then we can conclude that if God is the center of your relationship, then your marriage will never fail."

The soft and heavenly melody of Phil Wickham's 'Beautiful' began playing, and Jonathan led me to the communion table. We bowed our heads and prayed for one another before partaking of the elements.

"Lord," Jonathan spoke quietly, "I just want to thank You so much for gifting me with Natasha. I pray that our marriage honors and glorifies You, and that our love for one another will grow deeper and deeper every day. Help me to be the leader she needs me to be. In Jesus' name, amen."

I smiled as I began. "Heavenly Father, I thank you as well for gifting me with Jonathan. I pray I can be the best helper to him, that I would support and encourage him, and show him great respect all the days of my life. That nothing would ever break us apart and that together, we would grow to be more and more like You. In Jesus' name, amen."

We lit the unity candle, and then Jonathan's warm hand held mine again as he walked me back to the altar.

We repeated the simple, yet special vows, and then gave each other our engraved, white-gold wedding bands. I read the verse engraved on mine, the one God gave Jonathan for me, Proverbs 31, and then Jonathan's, Isaiah 43:19-21. This will be a constant reminder—even in hard times—that God wanted us to be husband and wife.

Pastor John looked at me. "Natasha, do you take Jonathan to be your lawfully wedded husband as long as you both shall live?"

I refrained from singing the words. "I do."

"Jonathan, do you take Natasha to be your lawfully wedded wife as long as you both shall live?"

He observed me, as if gazing into my soul. "I do."

Pastor John faced our family and friends and delivered his parting words. "I pronounce, by the authority vested in me by the State of Florida, but more importantly, by the Holy Spirit of God, that Jonathan and Natasha are a couple in Christ and by the name of the Father, the Son and the Holy Spirit, what God has joined together, let no man separate." He turned to us and grinned. "Jonathan, you may now kiss your bride."

Jonathan and I stepped forward like two magnets drawn to the other. His hand cradled my cheek, and his soft lips met mine. And with the kiss of a life time, I became his wife, and he became my husband.

epilogue

As of this writing, Jonathan and I have been married for over twelve years, and it has truly been wonderful. Not perfect, but wonderful. I 100 percent attribute that to Jesus Christ. His love sustains us. His love guides and teaches us, and draws us closer and closer, as we draw ourselves to Him.

I don't know where you're at right now in life, but I know this, Jesus is constant. His love doesn't falter or wane, His wisdom never dims, His patience is long-suffering, and His plans are always good for those who love Him and are called according to His purposes.

Sometimes, we are not where we think we want to be, or even know we should be. But God's grace can redirect, and He is able to provide a way where there is no way. Everything you read testifies of that. I wrote this story down the first year I got married. The memories were so fresh in my mind. I was the kind of girl who would relay every detail to my friends about my love interests, Marilyn and Alice can testify.

I hope and pray my story, and Jonathan's story, and Natalia's story has encouraged you to see just how good God is and that He is worthy to be trusted.

I also pray if you're single, or even in a relationship, that God has used what He did in our lives to give more clarity on His desires for you in this area. The Bible tells us not to be unwise, but to know what the will of the Lord is (Ephesians 5:17).

Relationships are so powerful. They have the power to build up, or to corrupt (1 Corinthians 15:33). Please do not take lightly who you give your time and your heart to, and that includes friends. Pray and seek God's wisdom for you as a child of His who desires to get married someday. He has all the answers and is able to provide them for you.

Until my next book, know that I've prayed for you, my precious reader, and the Unseen One sees you.

Love,

Natasha

Sign up to my newsletter to stay tuned for
more bookish news:
www.NatashaSapienza.com